LORD TEDRIC

LORD TEDRIC

E. E. DOC SMITH
with
GORDON EKLUND

BARONET PUBLISHING COMPANY, NEW YORK

LORD TEDRIC

A Baronet Book

First Baronet edition published September 1978

Copyright © 1978 by Baronet Publishing Company and Verna Smith Trestrail

ISBN: 0-89437-021-9

Baronet Publishing Company
509 Madison Avenue
New York, N. Y. 10022

LORD TEDRIC

1 FIST-BOXING

he blond swordsman treads cautiously forward. Over-head, the eye of a red sun gleams with the faint light of a tired flame. A bleak, blasted, cratered landscape, its te-dium interrupted only by the twisted skeletal remains of a single tree, stretches away from the swordsman on all sides. A hot wind, choked with black dust, burns at his eyes and lips. The swordsman draws his iron weapon free of its sheath. He moves relentlessly now. Gray eyes squint to see the first sign of an approaching enemy.

The swordsman thinks: I am Lord Tedric of the Marshes. I am warrior-king of all civilized Lomarr. If I fall this day, if I perish in this hell, the world will long remember my glory.

But he must not fall. He must not die. The obliteration of the ancient curse of black wizardry lies too near at hand. A few more steps. A few more passes of the longsword. The forbidden castle of Sarpedion stands ahead, beyond the un-seen horizon. He will fight on. He will emerge triumphant.

*He will rule as Lord Tedric, first Emperor of the Human
World.*

*Then, suddenly, they are upon him. The hordes of
Sarpedion rise from the broken land like a plague of insects.
Tedric lifts his sword and prepares to meet their assault.
The odds against him are one hundred to one.*

Yet he will win.

He must.

Phillip Nolan, a senior cadet at the Imperial
Academy of the Corps of the One Hundred on the
artificial planet Nexus in the heart of the Empire of
Man, leaned back in his chair and raised a gloved
hand to shield his eyes against the fierce glare of the
overhead lights. A meter and a half from where he
sat, in the center of the ropes of a square ring, two
men dressed from head to toe in heavy steel stalked
one another like lumbering beasts in a savage jungle.
Suddenly, the larger of the two men lashed out.
There was a ring of steel striking steel. The second
man struggled to pedal back. The other lunged forward, swinging again. *Clang.* Again, he swung.

"Like to place a wager, sir?" asked Traynor, Phillip Nolan's personal manservant, who stood beside his
chair. "I'll stand you five-to-one the big fellow flattens
him inside three minutes."

Nolan shook his head. "Your salary is already too
large, Traynor. I have no wish to fatten it." The
larger of the boxers, Nolan recalled, was known as
Tedric. If he had another name—a family name—

Nolan was not aware of it. "The only reason the bout has lasted this long is that Tedric's being kind."

"From pity, do you think?"

Nolan shrugged. "Let's call it mercy."

Another loud ringing clang drew Nolan's attention back to the ring. Tedric had backed his opponent, a native Earther named Dani Bayne, into a corner. The armored men stood toe-to-toe, flaying at one another with steel fists, but Tedric threw a half-dozen punches in return for every one he received. Nolan knew it was only a matter of time now—and not much time at that. Tedric hit Bayne on top of the head. *Clang.* Bayne sagged. Tedric hit him in the chest. *Clang.* The jaw. The chest again, then an uppercut to the face. Bayne seemed to rise a full centimeter off the floor. Tedric stepped back, lowered his arms, and watched as Bayne hit the floor with a conclusive thud.

Nolan let out a whistle of admiration. "That was damned impressive." The rest of the audience, the combined senior and junior classes of the Academy, nearly three hundred men, applauded loudly, but Nolan failed to join them. He stared at the fallen Bayne and slowly shook his head. "That Tedric is as good a boxer as any I've seen," he told Traynor.

"And Bayne defeated every opponent in the tournament easily until now."

"He could beat me."

"Tedric?"

"No, Bayne."

The referee, an ancient one-armed veteran of the Wykzl War, counted the final toll above Bayne. In a corner, convinced no doubt that the fight was over, Tedric removed his armored helmet. Although his pale face and blond hair were streaked with sweat, he barely seemed to be breathing hard. He shook off his gloves, wiped his face with the back of a hand, and reached down to unfasten the metal plates that covered his chest.

"I think I'll shake his hand," Nolan said, standing impulsively.

"But, sir, your own bout—"

"Let it wait for Carey. I'll be back."

As he leaped into the ring, Nolan tried to recall what little he knew of this man Tedric. Naturally, he had noticed him—at a height of two meters, Tedric was a very noticeable man—but despite nearly two years together at the Academy, Nolan could not remember exchanging a word with Tedric. He was the class mystery man, with no friends and few acquaintances; rumors concerning his origins had circulated since the very first days. Nolan seldom paid much attention to such tales, but nonetheless he did sometimes wonder. Who was this man? What was he doing here at the Academy among the tired remnants of the noblest families of the once magnificent Empire of Man?

Tedric was smoothing the creases in his pale blue senior class uniform when Nolan approached. Glancing up, Tedric's eyes showed a peculiar fusion of arrogance and uncertainty. "What do you want?" he said coldly.

Nolan tried a grin. "Nothing more than to say congratulations." Reaching out, he took Tedric's hand between both of his and shook. "I want to say that I've never seen such a display in all of my life. You're going to win this tournament, you know. There isn't a one of us who can touch you."

"Winning is a possibility." Tedric spoke with an underlying air of hesitancy, as if Galactic were not his native language. But that was impossible for *any* human being—wasn't it?

"I'd call it a hell of a lot more than that," Nolan said. "You've got only one more man to whip—either me or Matthew Carey."

There was a flash of something—could it be anger?—in Tedric's eyes at the mention of Carey's name, but it quickly subsided. He shrugged. "The best man will win."

"Ah, yes. Yes, of course. So they say, but—" Nolan seldom felt at a loss for words, but this was one of those rare occasions. Talking to Tedric was like pulling elephants' teeth. "I'm afraid I missed your preliminary bouts. How did they go?"

"I won."

"By knockout?"

"Yes."

Nolan let his grin become a laugh. "That's fantastic. Incredible. When I win, it's usually because the other guy gets tired chasing me around the ring and decides to take a snooze to rest. You nearly killed poor Bayne."

"That was not my intention," Tedric said stiffly.

It was plain to Nolan that Tedric had little interest in further conversation, even if he'd held much interest to begin with, which Nolan rather doubted. He started to say something else, thought better of it, shrugged inwardly, then made a polite bow. "Perhaps we will see each other again before graduation."

"It is quite possible certainly."

"Oh, you mean in the tournament final?" Nolan laughed. "I'm afraid there's no way I can whip Carey."

"Nonetheless, I wish you luck."

"You do?" Nolan couldn't conceal his surprise—and pleasure. "Well, I thank you for that."

As he crossed the ring, as confused and intrigued as when he'd first gone to speak to Tedric, Nolan spotted Traynor hurrying to intercept him. He paused and waited.

"Sir, surely you can't have forgotten that you fight next."

"I haven't forgotten, no." Nolan turned and glanced at Tedric, who was now leaving the ring. "I just wish I could."

"You can whip him, sir. I know you can."

"And you're a liar, Traynor. I know you are." Tedric was leaving the auditorium. His departure raised an odd mixture of emotions in Nolan: disappointment that Tedric had not stayed to see him fight and relief that he had not stayed to see him lose. Nolan turned and held out his hands to Traynor. "All right, dress me," he said. "Let's prepare the poor lamb for the slaughter."

Later, in his corner, burdened down by forty pounds of armored plate, Nolan waited impatiently for his opponent, Matthew Carey, to arrive. "Isn't this just like Carey?" he said. "He must be trying to heighten the drama by making everyone sit on their hands and wait."

"What did you discuss with that odd young man Tedric?" Traynor asked.

Nolan couldn't tell if he was really interested or merely trying to divert attention from the impending bout.

"I couldn't say we discussed much of anything. I told him how much I admired his abilities. He told me I had a chance to beat Carey."

"That was nice of him."

"I don't think he was trying to be nice."

"No, he's a strange one for sure. There's a rumor —I don't know if you've heard it or not, sir—that he has some connection with the Scientists."

Nolan had heard that rumor. It was all anyone had ever talked about for two years in connection with Tedric. "I first heard that rumor a week after we arrived here."

"And is it true?"

Nolan struggled to shrug his shoulders past the bulk of the armor he wore. "I'd be the last to know either way. The Scientists don't confide in me."

Traynor laughed—too loud. It was the usual sort of laughter a servant made in reply to one of his master's weak jokes. Nolan decided it was time to be serious. After all, maybe Tedric was right—maybe there was some way of beating Matthew Carey. Nolan had been trying every since he and Carey were big enough to stand on their own feet. Nolan had fought fairly and unfairly, clean and foul, viciously and kindly, mean and sly. He had lost every time. Still, there might be a way. Hadn't the ancients a saying: the strength of a pure heart is greater than the strength of a dozen foul ones? Nolan didn't know if his heart was pure; he knew Carey's sure as hell wasn't.

A rustle in the crowd below made Nolan turn his helmeted head. Through a narrow doorway at the far end of the auditorium, a tall figure dressed in black lumbered slowly into the room. Nolan knew at once who it finally had to be—Matthew Carey. He frowned at the sight of the soaring blue eagle, the Carey family crest, inscribed on the chest of the armored suit.

"I'll beat him to death," Nolan murmured. "I swear I will." But, even as he spoke, he knew that would not be true.

Carey approached the ring through the crowd. There was a polite smattering of applause. No cadet in the Academy actually liked Carey, but none of them wanted him to guess that they did not. Despite an obvious attempt at trudging like a man weighted down, Carey moved his feet with unexpected ease. Nolan thought there just might be something fishy about that suit of black armor. A new alloy, he guessed, something lighter than steel. That was just like Matthew Carey, too. He was a man who left little to chance.

A trio of female servants, each dressed in a silver thigh-length gown emblazoned with the Carey family eagle, assisted Carey through the ropes. The presence of women at the Academy stood in strict defiance of the ancient code of the Corps. Nolan had raised a lone protest when Carey first moved the women into his quarters the previous year, but it was futile. There was little anyone or anything could do when faced with the desire of a Carey to have his or her own way. Legalities did not matter; the Careys wrote their own laws.

Nolan pushed Traynor away, then lumbered forward to meet Carey at center ring. He felt fat and bloated compared to the surety and grace with which Carey moved. The referee brought them together and spoke quickly regarding the rules of the game. Nolan forced himself to meet Carey's rigid gaze. It wasn't the arrogance in those pale disembodied eyes peeping through the narrow slit in the black helmet that disturbed him; it was the amusement. Carey was laughing at him—laughing with the supreme confidence of one who knows full well that the universe is nothing more than a private plum ripe for the plucking.

"Now please shake hands," the referee said, "go
to your corners, and may the better man win."

"I expect I will," Carey said mockingly. He thrust
out a hand. "Shall we shake on that, Phillip?"

"No, we shall not." Nolan turned his back and
hurried away with as much dignity as the weight of
his armor would permit. Behind, he could hear Carey's rich laughter filling the dead silence of the big
room.

"You perhaps shouldn't have done that, sir,"
Traynor said, from behind the ropes. "It won't look
like good form in the eyes of your classmen."

"They only wish they had my guts," Nolan said.

"You shouldn't let him irritate you that way."

"It's not irritation, Traynor. It's something more.
That man won't rest until he's humiliated me and my
family to the point where none of us will be able to
raise our heads above our navels. I won't let him do
that, Traynor. He can beat me up a hundred times a
night and I won't."

The bell rang.

As soon as he went forward to meet Carey, Nolan
felt his anger evaporate. Whom was he trying to kid?
Pride was one thing, but defeat was something else.
He had refused to shake hands with Carey. Carey was
going to win this fight. Which, in the long run, was
the greater humiliation?

Still, he would try. He always tried.

Carey danced swiftly forward to meet him.

The sport of armored fist-boxing had long since

abolished the traditional concept of a limited number of rounds of a specific duration. After the opening bell, a bout continued until one fighter failed to regain his feet after a count of ten seconds. Despite this, serious injuries were very rare, and the blame for most of these lay with faulty equipment. Nolan knew that the worst that could happen to him today was defeat, but defeat was terrible enough in itself.

He decided to swing first.

As he raised his right arm, straining against the weight of the armor, he saw Carey's laughing eyes. The sight only enraged him, so that he swung twice as hard as planned, which was a mistake. Long before his fist swept home, Carey was gone. Nolan's hand whistled through the empty air, and the force of the blow carried him out and down. He felt his feet slipping from under him and knew he was falling. He tried to throw out his hands to blunt the force of the fall, but the weight of his arms made that impossible. He hit the canvas flat on his face and lay there, struggling to breathe.

The referee began a hesitant count: "One . . . two . . . three . . . "

Nolan sensed Carey standing above. "Shut up," Carey told the referee. "That was a slip. Make him get up. I want to hit him once."

Nolan could hear the audience's laughter. Blinking away frustrated tears, he fought to his knees. "You're cheating," he told Carey. "Your armor is made from something besides steel."

"There's nothing in the rules about steel. You can quit if you want, Nolan. Otherwise, start fighting."

Nolan gritted his teeth. Carey was taunting him, and he knew he couldn't afford another wild angry punch like that last one. He forced himself to be calm. Fists raised, he trudged forward, driving Carey in front of him. He would try to pin him in a corner. Carey unleashed a series of swift left hands. Nolan took them on his steel fists. The blows barely stung. Nolan started to think. What if the lightness of Carey's armor extended to his fists as well? He could move fast but not punch hard. There might be a real advantage there. If I catch him, I'll kill him, Nolan thought.

Carey seemed unaware. He pedaled back, letting Nolan carry the right, flicking an occasional left hand. The corner was nearby.

Another meter and I've got him, Nolan thought. Victory is mine at last.

Carey stopped in apparent surprise when his spine touched the corner ropes. He made an effort to slip free, but Nolan planted both feet and refused to budge. One punch, he thought, and that will be it. If I miss, I'll never catch him again.

Nolan let his right fist fly.

But, as he did, Carey also moved. He lifted his right arm in a wide arc. The fist sped through the air. Even as it fell, Nolan understood. A trick. The diversionary left hand. The right, poised in readiness, created from a substance not only lighter but also tougher than steel. He knew he was beat before Carey's right hand smashed the crown of his helmet. His head felt squeezed to the size of a peanut. He reeled, seeing black, then bright red. He fell. He never felt himself hit, never heard the referee's count.

When he awoke, Nolan saw the empty helmet on the canvas beside his head. Straining to see, he made out Traynor's concerned face hanging in apparent midair.

The auditorium was silent and empty.

Nolan shut his eyes.

But even here, in private darkness, he still saw Matthew Carey's taunting eyes, heard his derisive laughter like the haunting cry of some great bird of prey.

Beaten, Phillip Nolan sat in his room and thought about the past.

Not much more than one hundred years ago, his family—the Nolan family—had stood at the pinnacle of power and privilege within the Empire of Man. No other family was nearly as famous, respected, or rich. Among his ancestors, Phillip Nolan could number three imperial counselors, two fleet admirals, and a half-dozen Corps commanders.

At this same time—approximately one century in the past—the Carey family occupied a small plot of land on an obscure world known as Milrod Eleven. The Careys were not rich, except perhaps by local standards, nor were they famous, and even their nearest neighbors saw no good reason to hold them in high respect.

So what had occurred within such a brief span of time to alter the situation so dramatically?

To the best of Phillip Nolan's knowledge, things had begun to change the day Fraken Carey managed to bribe enough credit to obtain his oldest son, a boy named Melor, an appointment to the Imperial Academy of the Corps of the One Hundred. Melor, probably the ablest and certainly the most deceitful of the Careys, had been graduated at the top of his class of cadets and rewarded with a commission as a brigade lieutenant under the command of the current Imperial Fleet Admiral, Tompkins Nolan. This was during the last days of the centuries-long Wykzl War, and after the final battle in space, when the Empire of Man at last met abject defeat, it was Melor Carey who returned to Earth a hero, victorious in a minor skirmish, while Tompkins Nolan was branded a failure or worse.

For Phillip Nolan, this was more than mere history—a formal collection of names, dates, and dim videographs. It was private and personal—his own fate intimately involved. The reasons behind the simultaneous rise of the Careys and fall of the Nolans lay bound up with the history of the Empire of Man over the past one hundred years. Largely, it was a matter of corruption. An expansive, thriving Empire created leaders of a similar sort, golden men to build a Golden Age. But the Empire of today—corrupt and decadent—required nothing more than what the Careys could give it—more of the same.

The Academy itself provided an easy example. A millennium past, at its founding, the Corps of the One Hundred had been a select guard, answerable to the Emperor alone, and limited in number to the one hundred best qualified individuals in the realm. Today, that same Corps had swollen to include a good five thousand officers, only a few of whom actually stood active duty. Commissions were regularly bought and sold; membership in the Corps was nothing more than a hollow sign of family status. It was something every rich man's son needed to have. Especially a Carey son.

Phillip Nolan knew that if he hated Matthew Carey—and he did—then one reason was simply jealousy. But he did not care. The feeling was something he could not control, nor did he wish to. When he'd first met Matthew Carey at the imperial school on Earth fifteen years ago when both were six, both boys had loathed each other on sight. Nolan knew he would gladly have given up an arm or an eye to have emerged victorious from his meeting with Carey in the fist-boxing tournament. Even now, beaten, he thought it might be worth several fingers to see Carey thrashed.

He wondered: if I cannot do it myself, then why not another? His thoughts turned toward the strange man, Tedric, and the methodical manner in which he had whipped poor Bayne. Tomorrow's final bout between Tedric and Carey promised to be a most interesting match indeed. Could Tedric possibly win? Nolan scratched his chin and suddenly grinned. Well, why not? he thought. Carey was a fine boxer—no arguing there—but he was hardly unbeatable. And Tedric was tough. Damned tough and damned strong. The idea of a man with no last name rising up to best the brightest of the Carey clan seemed incongruous. Incongruous, yes, thought Nolan, but not necessarily impossible.

He stood up. Traynor slept nearby, but Nolan made no attempt to disturb him. Quietly, he opened the door and tiptoed into the corridor. He had made a decision. If he couldn't beat Carey on his own, he could still do everything in his power to ensure that someone else did. He would visit Tedric and warn him personally of Carey's new armor.

Did Tedric want his help? Nolan didn't know the answer to that, nor did he particularly care. Whether wanted or not, help was what Tedric was about to receive. He must win tomorrow's fight. The dignity of the Nolan name depended on that. The dignity of a family and the honor of an empire.

Phillip Nolan had already succeeded in convincing himself of all that.

2 MYSTERY MAN

The blond warrior, Tedric, swings his longsword relent-lessly back and forth, chopping at arms and legs, slicing throats and thighs, like a farmhand harvesting a field of wheat. A dozen men lie dead at his feet, two dozen. Still they come and still he fights. Blood drips from a hundred minor wounds sprinkled across his huge frame. Tedric ignores the pain. His thoughts are focused far from such worldly suffer-ings. He thinks of Sarpedium, the black wizard, and the pain and anguish he has wrought upon the world for untold centuries. Tedric is not immortal. No magical potions or secret elixirs protect him from death's dark hand. At any moment, an enemy may slip past his guard and strike him a fatal blow. Yet Tedric battles on, oblivious to fear, driven by the unwavering need to make the world right and by the fierce belief that only he can accomplish this act of salvation.

And so, in time, the hordes of Sarpedion, thoroughly beaten, withdraw from the field of battle, vanishing into the mist as mysteriously as they first appeared. Tedric rests then.

23

Sitting on the warm earth, he balances his bloodstained sword between his knees. His breath comes fast. He has won again. But this was a battle—the war itself is far from done.

As had happened nearly every night for the past two years, as soon as the banks of artificial light that passed for daytime on Nexus grew dim, Tedric turned to the far wall of his room, removed an armload of books from the shelves located there, and began the slow, laborious, hateful process of reading and memorizing.

He knew this wasn't for him. Studying was not a simple task. There was too much to learn and too little time in which to comprehend it all. There was history, mathematics, the bionomics of a hundred planets and the physics of a thousand systems. Tedric, unlike his fellow cadets, had not entered the Academy with the benefit of a dozen previous years of formal education. He could read and write common Galactic—the Scientists had seen to that—but otherwise, awash among all these books, he felt as comfortable as a naked man abandoned in the land of the fully clothed. He was a man of action, not of words, and here at the Academy of the Corps of the One Hundred, words seemed to count for at least as much as mere actions.

Already, even as he began to study, the black squiggles that represented words on the white pages of the book began to weave and flutter as if they were live, tiny insects. Tedric blinked, rubbed his eyes, tried again to read. There were, of course, many quicker ways of mastering a subject than reading and remembering. There were machines that talked, pills to aid memorization, holographic tapes that brought the lecturer right into the room and let him answer specific questions. Tedric had at one time or another attempted to use all these devices, but such technology always made him uncomfortable and he returned to the one sure method he preferred above the others: reading books. For hours and hours at a time. Till his head throbbed, his eyes burned. But it had worked—after a fashion. Now, as his two years at the Academy drew to a close, he stood somewhere near the middle of his class in academic achievement. It was a surprise. An unexpected victory. But the Scientists had told him how important a high ranking was and, for Tedric, that was enough. He always obeyed the Scientists' orders. They had brought him here. Given him life. How could he fail to do as they demanded?

A persistent knocking at the door to the room distracted Tedric. Puzzled—he received few if any visitors, especially so late at night—he laid down his book and went to answer. His room was an impersonal domicile, little disturbed since the day he'd moved in. There was a cot, a metal desk and chair, a broken computer receiver, one small rug, and of course the books—several hundred of them. Tedric did not think of this place as a home. It was merely a resting station, a certain space occupied for a set period of time. Tedric had had a real home once—the faint memory of such a place occasionally stirred in his dreams—but that was long ago and far away and could never be glimpsed in full again.

The figure standing on the opposite side of the door was a faintly familiar man dressed in the pale blue uniform of a senior cadet. A classmate. Nolan. Phillip Nolan. The family name was familiar to Tedric through his classes in imperial history. But that was true of many of his classmates.

He bowed stiffly. "I am Tedric, at your service."

"Yes—yes, I know." Nolan seemed oddly nervous. His eyes darted. "I'm Nolan. Phillip Nolan."

"You wish to speak with me?" Tedric prodded.

"I . . . yes." Turning his head, Nolan peered swiftly down the corridor, as if fearing that some unknown observer might be watching. "May I come in? I promise not to take up much time. This is important."

Tedric shrugged. He knew he needed the time in which to study, but the diversion was not exactly unwelcome. Drawing back, he let Nolan pass, then closed the door and, for a reason he could not quite articulate, bolted the lock as well.

Nolan, searching for a place to sit, finally dropped tensely to the edge of the bed. "You and I have been classmates for nearly two years now, but I don't think we've exchanged a dozen words."

"I know few of you well," Tedric said, "though we did talk today. I remember you came over and congratulated me on my victory over Bayne."

"Yes, and I meant that. I really did. It was an extraordinary performance."

Tedric shrugged. "I understand you had less luck yourself later on."

Nolan grinned shamefully. "I don't think luck had anything to do with it. You see, that's partially why I'm here. It's about your fight—your final match tomorrow with Matthew Carey. I wanted to give you a warning. Carey has a trick. A special suit of armor. It's light—he moves like a snake—but tough. He nearly took my head off with one punch."

"And you came here to inform me of this trick?" Tedric could not conceal his suspiciousness. He trusted no one in this world, especially a man with a name as famous as Nolan's. "Why?"

"Because . . . because . . . well, frankly, because I loathe Matthew Carey. Nothing would make me happier than seeing him get knocked on his rear."

"And you wish to use me as your agent? So that I can accomplish what you failed to perform on your own?"

Nolan's shamefaced smile returned. "I wouldn't put it that bluntly," he said, "but it's true. I just wanted to be sure that you'd have an equal chance. Now that you know what Carey's up to, you can plan a defense of your own."

"And you have a suggestion as to how to proceed?" Tedric sat down beside the desk. He was biding for time. It was something about that name—Phillip Nolan. It had suddenly come to him that he had heard it before and not in any history book.

"Well, I'm no strategist," Nolan said, "but if I were you, I know what I'd do. I'd play dumb. Dumb and slow. I'd let Carey back me into a corner, blocking only enough punches to keep me on my feet. I'd let him catch the scent. Carey is cocky. He thinks he can lick the world. I'd let him get to thinking that and then I'd hit him. I've seen your hands. One good punch wouldn't necessarily put him out, but it would fluster him. He'd panic, run. Then you could put him out. I really believe you could."

"So do I," Tedric said. He had remembered now where he had heard Phillip Nolan's name before. There was only one possible place. On Prime. The Scientists had told him about Nolan and, like so much of the information they had given him, it had been forgotten until now. "But I won't do it."

Nolan's face registered shock, then anger, and finally bitterness. He looked like a man betrayed. Standing, his arms clenched stiffly at his sides, he said, "Do I understand you to say that you intend to lose that match tomorrow on purpose?"

"Something like that." Tedric jerked his head at the bed. "If you'll sit down, I'll—"

"No!" Nolan said angrily. "Don't explain. I'm not stupid. I can put four and four together and get eight. Matthew Carey is the scion of the most powerful family in the Empire. Beat him in a fight, humiliate him in front of his peers, and you risk your own imperial career. All right, I'm sorry. I thought because you were someone different, someone without the handicap of a last name, you might not be afraid of Carey. I see I was wrong. And I apologize for that. I really do."

"Wait!" Tedric said. His voice cracked like a whip.

Nolan froze, startled by the strength of command in Tedric's tone. Slowly, he turned. "Why—why should I?"

"Because you didn't bother to let me explain why I'm losing. You see, it's not really my idea, Nolan. I dislike losing as much as any man. It was the Scientists. They told me to lose, and I intend to obey their wishes."

Nolan glared. "That's the most absurd story I've heard in my life."

Tedric clenched his teeth, fighting the anger that welled up. "I am not a liar," he said, with a calmness that surprised him.

"Then those stories about you—they weren't made up? You have been in contact with the Scientists? They really do exist?"

"I lived on their planet—on Prime—for some months."

"And they sent you here?"

"They assisted in obtaining my appointment, yes."

Nolan whistled softly. He had apparently made up his mind not to go away, after all. He sat on the edge of the bed again. "I do wish I'd been present when the Commandant received that call. The expression on his face would have been a lovely thing indeed. But tell me. What do they look like? The Scientists, that is. Are they like the biomen, or are they completely human?"

Tedric tried to remember. Nothing of his time on Prime ever came clearly to him. "Human—I think."

"And they sent you all this way to lose a fight to Matthew Carey?" The skepticism had returned to Nolan's voice.

Tedric pretended not to notice. "That's just one little thing."

"Then what's the big thing?"

"I don't know," Tedric admitted, momentarily confused.

"You don't know?" Nolan repeated, with no attempt at concealing his astonishment.

"Not completely. Not definitely. I was given certain orders, instructions buried in my memory that emerge only in the face of specific stimuli. Your visit here tonight. The Scientists told me about you."

"And what did they say?"

"That I should confide in you. Trust you."

"Such as?"

"Well, for instance, who I am. Nobody here knows that. I wasn't born in this universe. I have certain memories, recollections; they usually come to me when I'm sleeping, dreaming. I see visions, landscapes and objects that do not exist anywhere here."

"How can you be sure?"

"Because I am." Tedric leaned against the desk, letting his huge hands support the bulk of his weight. He knew there was no way he could put into words the sights he had seen, the different geometries, shapes, textures. "There is one thing, though, that I do remember very well, and that's my awakening on Prime. I wasn't a child. I was an adult, the same as you see me now. And that was my birth. I remember nothing clearly from before."

"And your friends, the Scientists, they wouldn't tell you?"

"They said there would come a time."

"When?"

"That they didn't say."

Nolan scratched his chin and sighed. "Look, let's face it, this is half-crazy. I came here to give you some advice about knocking out a man I don't happen to like. You said no, which was your right, but now all of a sudden we're talking about the Scientists, whom I never believed in, and different universes and crazy things like that. Do you really expect me to believe what you say?"

"I don't care. Believe me or don't—that's your business. The Scientists suggested I talk to you. Now I have."

"But, damn it, the Scientists don't know me."

"Are you so sure? The Scientists know a great deal more than most of us can guess."

"Can they predict the future?"

"They say they can't. What they do is foresee the probability of certain events, but the actual future remains an unknown quantity until it has become the present."

The information seemed to please Nolan. "Then they have no way of knowing if you and I will ever see each other again, which isn't very likely, after graduation."

"That's true."

Nolan pursed his lips, lost in sudden thought. Finally, he stood, extending a hand, which Tedric accepted. "Let's put it this way," Nolan said. "I'm not convinced and I'm not unconvinced, but if you're just telling a story, then it's the wildest one I've ever heard. Tomorrow, when you fight Carey, I'll just hide in my room. I'll cover my ears and pretend the fight has never happened. Then I'll wait. You see, after graduation, I intend to accept an active commission. I'm the youngest son in my family and there's really nothing for me anywhere else. I assume you'll be doing the same. When our assignments are granted, on graduation day, if yours and mine turn out to be the same—and I suppose the chance of that is pretty slim—then I promise to take your story very seriously. Fair enough?"

Tedric nodded. "Of course. If you want it that way." He escorted Nolan to the door, unbolted the lock, and let him into the dim corridor. He said goodbye, but it wasn't farewell. He would see Phillip Nolan again. He was convinced of that—absolutely. The

Scientsists had told him, and the Scientists were never wrong.

Some twenty-seven days (each day being a quantity of time equal to the rotational period of the Earth) subsequent to the crowning of Matthew Carey as fist-boxing champion of the senior cadet class, the one hundred fourteen members of the one thousand, four hundred, ninety-first graduating class of the Imperial Academy of the Corps of the One Hundred gathered in Kimball Hall, a spherical room located at the very core of Nexus, to receive their commissions as officers. The blue-uniformed senior cadets sat in circular rows that sloped away from the central point of the hall, each row slightly higher than the ones in front of it.

Tedric sat in the first row, which included the five highest ranking members of the class, a position he had achieved more by physical prowess than academic achievement. Matthew Carey sat to his immediate left, while in front of them, at the low central point of the hall, stood the Academy Commandant, Flin Marson, a decorated veteran of the Wykzl War, a man of at least one hundred thirty years. Marson recited the words of the traditional graduation address, the same words first uttered more than a thousand years ago before the initial graduating class, and even though he had been required to learn the speech by heart, Tedric managed to listen with some interest. What he sought was some firm clue, something to help him understand the past glory and present decline not only of the Corps of the One Hundred but of the Empire it served.

". . . to serve and assist wherever possible the intelligent creatures of the civilized Galaxy, our emperor has ordained the establishment of this elite corps of one hundred male human beings. Those of you chosen to go forth will serve not merely as representatives of the Emperor but as true extensions of his personal power and glory. For you to fail as individuals, to bring disgrace upon yourselves, is to bring that same disgrace upon the crown of the Emperor. Your responsibility, therefore, is a vast one, but the authority granted you is equally immense. Do not fail your emperor. Do not fail your corps. And, above all, do not fail yourselves. I can ask nothing more of you than that. The future of civilization depends upon your keen judgment."

Tedric, leaning forward to hear better since the aging Commandant Marson spoke in a soft whisper, heard Matthew Carey let out a snicker of contempt. Marson must have heard also, for he glanced up suddenly and showed a pained expression on his face. Although Marson said nothing and soon resumed reciting, Tedric thought that in that quick, silent expression of hurt and anguish, he might have learned something important. The Corps as it existed today could not be confused with the Corps of a thousand or even a hundred years ago. When Marson evoked such concepts as dignity, civilization, and keen judgment, he was speaking more to men long since dead than to those gathered in this room. Tedric understood that what had happened could largely be blamed upon the war. If there was one thing he had learned during his two years at the Academy, it was the stunning effect upon mankind of its defeat at the hands of the alien Wykzl.

Marson continued to recite. "So I charge you finally with these parting words: do right, do good, be bold, be strong. And, if you follow these simple precepts, you must in the end succeed, and with your success, the Empire of Man will continue to thrive as a civilized institution, much as it has since man's first hesitant steps beyond the realm of his ancient home."

There was a scattering of applause, which Tedric joined, but most of the handclapping stopped as soon as it became apparent that Matthew Carey intended to sit with his hands folded. Phillip Nolan, seated in the row behind Tedric, continued to applaud long after everyone else had stopped.

Commandant Marson seemed embarrassed by this mixed reception. Hastily, he went on: "I will now read in order the names of those selected by our emperor, Kane IV, as officers in the Imperial Corps. Those of you designated for immediate active duty will be informed of your assignments at this time. When your name is called, please step forward and receive your commission. Matthew Carey." Marson spoke this name with unconcealed distaste.

Carey, moving languidly, left his seat and went

forward. He accepted his commission, bowed to the assembly, cocked a hand over his eye, and grinned.

Commandant Marson called the next name: "Tedric."

Tedric went forward. As he did, he felt the eyes of his fellow cadets watching intently and knew what they must be thinking. Who is this man? they wondered. How did he manage to finish second, higher than me, in the total class standings?

Tedric accepted the yellow parchment from Commandant Marson and also received a folded sheet of white paper—his assignment orders. He shook Marson's hand, then turned deliberately around and faced the rows of seats. "None of you know me," he said, choosing his words carefully and speaking with crisp authority, "and few of you ever will. You don't know who I am, where I've come from, or what I'm doing here. I just want to make you a promise. Even though I'm a stranger, this commission means something to me." He held up the yellow parchment and let it flutter in the dead air. "I won't disgrace it or what it stands for. That's a promise from me to you. And when I make a promise, I'm in the habit of making sure it sticks."

In surprised silence, Tedric went back to his seat. As soon as he dropped down, Matthew Carey leaned over and whispered softly, "I couldn't have put it any better myself." There was no trace of embarrassment or mockery in his tone.

"Then why didn't you?" Tedric didn't think he and Carey had ever exchanged a word before. Even during their fight, both men had remained silent.

"I'm not one for making speeches," Carey said. He held out his hand. "Mind if I take a look at your assignment orders?"

Tedric shrugged and handed Carey the sheet of folded paper he had received. Meanwhile, Commandant Marson continued to call the roll of graduating cadets.

Carey laughed pleasantly and handed back the paper. "Take a look at it yourself," he suggested. "It's what I knew it had to be. The *Eagleseye,* the biggest cruiser in the entire imperial navy. That's where I'm headed, too."

"You're entering active duty?" Tedric said, unable to conceal his surprise.

"Sure," Carey said. "Why not? I'm nobody special. I'm not somebody's fat son who buys a commission in the Corps just so he can hang it on a wall."

"I never meant to imply that you were."

"Sure, you didn't." Carey leaned closer, and his voice took on an almost conspiratorial tone. "What do you know about the *Eagleseye?*"

Tedric shook his head. Phillip Nolan had received his commission and returned to his seat. Tedric could sense him trying to eavesdrop. "All I know is what you just told me."

"My father had it built," Carey said. "That's why it's called what it is. The eagle is an extinct bird that once lived on old Earth. It's our family crest—our private symbol." Carey suddenly winked. "But do you know where it's headed? The *Eagleseye,* I mean."

Tedric glanced at his orders and shook his head. "It doesn't seem to say here."

"It can't. The matter is very much a secret. But I can tell you. There's a planet called Evron Eleven. The slaves there are attempting to rebel against legal authority. My father—the Emperor, too—they want me to head a party to go out and take care of the matter. It was my decision to let a few of my classmates go along. I think it ought to be an interesting way to start our careers."

"But there are no slaves in the Empire of Man."

Carey chuckled. "Call them workers, then." He drew away, pretending to listen to the Commandant's roll call. Tedric knew enough about Carey to realize that he wasn't the type of person who engaged in idle talk. What was all this about? he wondered. What was really happening on Evron Eleven?

Since there was no immediate way of answering these questions, Tedric decided to ignore them. He, too, pretended to listen as the names of the last of the one hundred fourteen graduating cadets were called.

When the last man had stepped forward and received his commission, Commandant Marson made no sign of dismissal. Instead, he shuffled his papers into a neat pile, then suddenly cleared his throat. When he spoke, there was a different tone to his voice, something tougher than anything Tedric had heard before.

"Men," said Marson, "that's it—that's all there is to it. You're all finished now, done. When you return to your quarters, you'll find a new silver uniform awaiting each one of you. Put it on. Wear it proudly. Other than that, I can say only one thing. If you fail, if you disgrace that uniform, whether you go out on assignment or sit at home and never move, I promise you'll pay. Maybe not now. Maybe not in my lifetime or even in yours. But the time will come. I guarantee it. And the reason I can say that—the reason I can be so sure—is because that uniform means a great deal more than most of you can ever hope to understand." As he spoke, Marson's gaze shifted until it seemed to fix upon Matthew Carey. "I don't mean to advise you or caution you. To be frank, I'm warning you. Watch what you do—watch out or, damn it, you'll pay." He lowered his voice and murmured, "Dismissed."

Tedric overheard Matthew Carey mutter, "The silly old fool," but anything further was lost beneath the noise of eagerly shuffling feet. Tedric tried to hurry out of the hall himself, but Phillip Nolan intercepted him at the door.

"I overheard you having a chat with Matthew Carey," Nolan said.

"He wanted to compare assignments. What do you think of what Commandant Marson said there at the end?"

Nolan shook his head. "I think it took a lot more nerve than I knew the old guy possessed."

"Because of Carey?"

"That's who he was talking to."

"Carey thought so, too. I heard him call Marson an old fool."

"And he may not be too far off at that. The poor

sap. This'll mean the end of it for him."

"Marson will be removed?"

"More than likely. You see, that's the whole point of what he was saying. The Corps has been about the last great imperial institution to hold out against the Careys. Matthew, I imagine, is supposed to change that. I'm sure it's why he's going on active duty. In ten years—maybe less—he intends to be running the whole show."

"And will he?"

Nolan shrugged. "I've never heard of anyone making money betting against the Careys so far."

"Then it's that bad."

"That bad—or worse. But that's not what I wanted to talk to you about. See this?" Nolan held up a sheet of paper. "It's my assignment."

After what Matthew Carey had told him, Tedric did not have to read what was written there. "The *Eagleseye*," he said.

"That's your assignment?" Nolan said.

"Mine and yours."

Nolan grinned. "Well, how about that? I guess we will be seeing a lot of each other from now on."

Tedric winked. "I told you so, didn't I?"

"You and your Scientists. Maybe I ought to think again about all you told me the other night."

"Maybe you should at that." Tedric gave a quick salute, then turned away in the direction that led toward his room.

3 EAGLESEYE

Tedric, the blond swordsman of Lomarr, pauses briefly in his pursuit of the black wizard, Sarpedium, to meet with another wizard, Corlock the Sly. Corlock, who is more than three thousand years old, lives in an underground cave at the edge of the blasted land where the castle of Sarpedium stands. The old wizard greets Tedric familiarly at the entrance to his home and asks that he sheath his sword before going inside.

"The weapon will do you no good here," says Corlock, "for my magic is capable of vanquishing any mortal weapon."

Tedric does not believe this assertion, for his sword has been forged from the new iron metal, but he abides by the wizard's request.

The two men sit beside the tall green flames of a fire that burns without wood. "So you are the mortal who was once an ironmaster and now intends to rid the world of magic and wizardry."

41

"My quarrel is with black magic and evil wizards only," says Tedric, who nonetheless reaches surreptitiously down and clutches the hilt of his sword.

"If Sarpedium falls before you, I fall, too."

"He is your eternal enemy."

"Mine, not yours. It is the same as the snake and the mongoose. If there were no snakes, the mongoose would die."

"The world is better rid of all wizards," Tedric says defiantly. *"Magic cheats those who do not know its secrets."*

"But with what will you replace it?"

"With science. With knowledge. With truth."

Corlock laughs an old man's laugh. *"You are a bold man, Tedric, but you are also a fool."*

"Time will tell the truth of that," says Tedric, standing.

Shaking his head in awe, Tedric turned away from the glorious porthole view of the massive silver ship spinning through space like an angel in heaven. "It is an impressive thing," he told Phillip Nolan, who had joined him at the porthole. "I wasn't aware even fleet cruisers were built that large."

Nolan seemed more irritated than impressed. "They weren't. And still shouldn't be. The *Eagleseye* is a Carey family pretension. It's huge and fantastic, but it's also wasteful and impractical. For war, it's nearly useless."

"But the Empire is no longer at war."

"Officially, no."

"The Wykzl have not penetrated your boundaries for a hundred years."

"There are more things in the Galaxy than the Wykzl alone."

"Are you speaking of some matter I am not aware of?"

Nolan shook his head and tried a smile. "No, not really. I guess what I mean is, for the past hundred years, we've become too complacent, too easily satisfied. It's as if, having lost a war and learned something of our limitations as a species, there's no longer any reason to worry about what might lie beyond. But I can't believe that. I don't think it's over. There's more to come, more to learn. It's the sight of things like that ship that bothers me."

"I've never heard you speak so seriously before, Phillip. Does the *Eagleseye* really disturb you so deeply?"

"It's a luxury. What's worse, it's a needless luxury I don't expect to enjoy serving on board."

"Especially with Matthew Carey as our operations officer."

Nolan frowned at the mention of the name. "You haven't seen him today, have you?"

"No, and like you, I'm beginning to wonder."

"No one's seen him since just after we first came on board."

"You don't think he could have left, do you?"

Nolan shook his head. "Where Carey's concerned, I try not to wonder about anything."

Tedric reached out and turned Nolan gently toward the open door behind them. "Come, Phillip, it must be nearly time to depart."

Nolan nodded slowly. "I suppose there's really no way out."

The subspace shuttle craft that carried Nolan and Tedric had been sent directly to Nexus in order to pick them up. It was now overcrowded to the point of bursting, and for that reason alone Tedric was glad that they had finally reached their destination, the orbiting hull of the *Eagleseye*. Every senior cadet assigned to active duty had received orders to board the *Eagleseye*, and once Nolan had learned of that, his skepticism concerning Tedric's story of the Scientists had returned. Still, Tedric refused to let that disturb him and when Nolan, surprisingly, had suggested that the two men share a cabin aboard the shuttle, he had eagerly agreed. The Scientists had directed him only to confide in Nolan; they had said nothing about making him believe the truth. Tedric knew from his two lonely years at the Academy how important it could be having a friend. Nolan, apparently, was more than willing to fit this bill.

The two men moved with practiced ease through the tight, narrow corridors of the shuttle. Even this brief voyage had given them time to acquire steady spacelegs prior to boarding the *Eagleseye*. It was largely a matter of gravity, Tedric believed. The centrifugal spin of even so large a ship as the *Eagleseye* never quite managed to equal the effect of native planetary gravity. When walking, it was necessary to learn the correct way of dipping the entire body, relaxing the spine and flexing the knees and thighs.

Most of the other cadets had already gathered around the enclosed area of the locks, even before Nolan and Tedric arrived. As Nolan moved away to chat with old friends, Tedric hung back, uncertain as always whether he ought to intrude. He quickly scanned the faces present and confirmed that Matthew Carey had still not put in an appearance. Most of the men seemed excited. Nolan had pointed out earlier that nearly all the cadets choosing active duty were younger sons. For them, this was a real adventure, something their more respectable older siblings would never have a chance to know. Tedric felt no pangs of nervousness himself. He had been through too much already in what seemed like a brief lifespan to let something as simple as a voyage through space at velocities far in excess of light disturb him.

The cadets, of course, were no longer that. They were true officers of the Corps now—lieutenants. Each wore the traditional silver suit of a corpsman emblazoned on each shoulder with large gold bars. At his waist, each man wore a holster, a heatgun on the right hip, and a sword and sheath on the left. The use of swords had surprised Tedric, but he had soon learned the reason behind the carrying of such an apparently antique weapon. The explosive nature of a heatgun made it impractical for use during close-quarter fighting aboard a ship. The beam could cut through even the hardest metal, and more than one corpsman had killed himself and all his men by using a heatgun without thinking of the possible results. A sword was not only safe, it was discriminating, and fencing was a staple element in the Academy curriculum.

The impact, when it came, caught Tedric totally by surprise. His knees buckled and he had to throw out a hand and grab the edge of the open doorway behind to keep from falling. Those cadets—or lieutenants—who also managed to keep their feet set off an immediate cheer. It took Tedric a moment to realize what had happened. The shuttle had banged into the hull of the *Eagleseye* and locked. In a moment, the doors would cycle open and they would be boarding the big cruiser.

Tedric turned to find Phillip Nolan standing at his shoulder. "Carey's still not here," he said.

"Perhaps he intends to board later. Surely, there will be time."

But Nolan shook his head. "I wonder," he said, wrinkling his brow in emphasis.

The massive bulk of the fleet cruiser *Eagleseye* seemed to dwindle as soon as the corpsmen stepped on board. The inner corridors proved to be even tinier than those of the shuttle—Tedric had to dip his head even to pass through them—while the staterooms were barely large enough for one man to turn around in it, much less two.

Nolan glared at the sailor who had escorted them to their room to show his displeasure. "Are you sure you haven't brought us to the wrong place?" he asked.

The sailor shook his head. "No, sir. If you think this is bad, you ought to see what they give us enlisted men. The rooms are hardly mugh bigger than this one, and there might be fifty or sixty of us crammed inside." The sailor, like most menial workers in the Empire, was a subman species originally created centuries ago from ancient Earth's more intelligent animal breeds. In this man's case, the bulk of his animal heritage was apparently some sort of cat. He had tan fur, eyes that were yellow slits, and a voice that seemed simultaneously to hiss and purr.

"It's hard to believe anything could be worse than this," said Tedric. The room contained two beds chained to the wall, a narrow strip of bare floor, and a tiny viewscreen located in one corner. Tedric shoved his meager belongings underneath the bottom bed and considered whether it was safe to attempt to sit. "The *Eagleseye* seems so huge when you first see it. Do you mean the crew is so large that this is all the room you can spare for guests?"

"That has nothing to do with it, sir," the sailor said. "It's not the regular crew, it's the N-space Drive. The way I understand it, the ship's so big it needs an engine ten times the normal size just to get up to N-velocities. At least three-quarters of our mass is made up by the engine. After that, there isn't a lot of room for human beings like us."

"Now do you understand what I meant?" Nolan told Tedric. "This is the Careys' private little boondoggle."

"It won't be a comfortable trip," Tedric agreed.

Before Nolan could go on, the viewscreen on the wall suddenly came to life. A pattern of bright lights flashed, then a voice said, "All incoming Corps personnel are instructed to report at once to the captain's lounge for a pre-voyage briefing. All boarding Corps personnel are instructed to report . . ."

Nolan reached out and slapped the screen and the voice immediately fell silent. "So soon?" he asked Tedric. "You'd think they'd give us time for a relaxing run through the vast expanses of our rooms."

The sailor intervened. "I can show you the way to the lounge, sirs."

"Then lead on," said Nolan, "whoever you are."

"Keller, sir. Assistant Steward Third-Class Keller."

"Then lead on, Mister Third-Class Keller."

The captain's lounge lay at the end of a maddening maze of rising, twisting, dipping corridors. Tedric had begun to despair of ever learning to find his way around the ship without assistance when Keller suddenly threw open a door, stuck his head inside, and announced, "Presenting the lieutenants, Nolan and Tedric."

The captain's lounge proved to be yet another small, poorly-lighted room. Enough chairs and couches had been scattered through its interior to provide seats for all the corpsmen, but aside from that, there was little room to stand or move around.

Nolan weaved his way toward an empty chair and beckoned to Tedric to join him. The other corpsmen looked up at their entry but said nothing. An aura of depression seemed to fill the room. Tedric looked at the tattered, torn upholstery of the furnishings and thought he understood. It was a matter of expectations. For such men as these, especially after their two-year hiatus at the Academy, the moment of entering into active service was something long anticipated. He knew what they must have expected to find: excitement, adventure, glory. So far, none had found anything greater than narrow corridors, dim rooms, torn furnishings. Tedric, who shared none of these anticipations, could only sympathize with the disappointment surrounding him. He guessed that Nolan must feel the same as the others but he, as usual, easily managed to conceal his true emotions beneath a cocky exterior.

Putting a finger through a hole in the arm of his chair, Nolan whispered to Tedric, "Maybe we ought to get our new fr'iend, Third-Class Keller, to repair this."

"Do you think he's actually assigned to us personally?"

Nolan shrugged. "I doubt it, but he seems to think so, and there's got to be hope in that. Life for me hasn't been the same since they sent poor old Traynor packing."

Tedric remembered with amusement how Nolan had complained long and hard at the Academy when the cadets' manservants were sent home alone.

The wait for the appearance of the captain proved to be a long one. Nolan reached into a pocket of his silver suit and drew out a packet of highly illegal tobacco, from which he offered Tedric a piece. When Tedric refused, Nolan tore off a mouthful and proceeded to chew. Tedric contented himself by studying the men around him. He sensed how greatly the situation had changed since the old Academy days and wanted to get a feel for where the men stood now. That, in fact, was really the substance of the alteration he sensed. These were indeed men now, no longer boys, and they had to be regarded as such.

Abruptly, without advance warning, a door in the rear of the room swung open, and a short, bulky, gray-faced man in a rumpled silver suit stepped through. He moved with the odd, loping gait of an experienced spacehand, and it took Tedric a long moment to realize that this rather inconsiderable figure must be the captain.

He didn't step far into the room. There wasn't enough space, with all the couches and chairs, to allow for that. A second figure followed the captain into the room, and Tedric saw Nolan's eyes grow wide with surprise. He soon understood why.

The second figure was Matthew Carey.

He stood directly behind the captain and, leaning close, whispered confidentially into his ear. The captain shook his head, Carey whispered some more, and this time the captain nodded compliantly.

"Gentlemen," said the captain, who seemed ill-at-ease and uncertain just how to proceed, "I want to be the first, as your captain, to welcome you aboard His Imperial Majesty's fleet cruiser, the *Eagleseye,* which as most of you no doubt know was originally designed and constructed by the factories of your fellow corpsman, Matthew Carey. Lieutenant Carey has, in fact, been my guest here aboard the *Eagleseye* for the past several days and during that time we have often discussed the details of the rather difficult mission presently facing us all. Lieutenant Carey has kindly consented to join me here today—" Nolan snorted audibly "—to help explain the exact nature of this assignment to you. Any questions you may have, once I have completed my initial briefing, may be directed either at me or at Lieutenant Carey."

Tedric knew that Nolan must be gnashing his teeth at this display of deference by the captain, but at least one minor mystery had been solved: the recent whereabouts of Matthew Carey. Obviously, since he had been seen leaving Nexus with the rest of the class, he must have slipped away from the shuttle sometime during the early stages of its voyage and taken a much faster ship to rendezvous ahead of everyone else with the *Eagleseye.* Why? That was the sort of question Tedric was not presently prepared to answer. He would watch and wait, solve the many mysteries surrounding him by experience alone.

"This is John Maillard," Carey put in, "and although he's an officer of the imperial fleet and not a corpsman, I'll expect each of you to pay him the proper respect due his rank, authority, and experience. Captain Maillard served with my paternal grandfather during the last sad days of the Wykzl War, and my own respect for his abilities and judgment is quite without bounds."

"Then why don't you show it by shutting your mouth?" Phillip Nolan muttered, in a voice loud enough to be overheard. Captain Maillard started to make an angry retort, but Carey shook his head and the captain fell silent.

In a moment, Captain Maillard went on. "I feel I should indicate at the very outset that your mission concerns a situation as critical as any the Empire has faced since the cessation of hostilities with the Wykzl. Lieutenant Carey has informed me that the planet Evron Eleven is one of the major sources within the Empire for the rare transuranic element, Dalkanium, which as most of you must know is an absolutely essential component fuel for the N-space Drive. Without a ready source of Dalkanium, all trade within the Empire would soon cease and with it an end to the civilized order that has taken centuries to create.

"The situation, simply, is this. The working classes on Evron Eleven, the majority of whom are submen brought at great expense from other worlds, have seized control of the mines and presently refuse to work unless a number of their demands are met. Lieutenant Carey, whose family holds a certain interest in the mines, tells me these demands are both unreasonable and treasonous. Put simply, what we face here is rebellion, an open challenge to imperial authority. I need not remind you that something such as this could very easily spread to the point where the Emperor himself might become a subject of ridicule within the precincts of his own realm. The fate of our empire, of civilization itself, may very well rest in your hands."

The captain's words, despite their surface drama, seemed to lack any real strength as he spoke them. Tedric wondered at once whether he was speaking from his own beliefs or whether his words might actually have been written out for him in advance. Was he speaking for Captain Maillard or was he speaking for Matthew Carey?

Tedric, apparently, wasn't the only one to wonder. Phillip Nolan raised his hand in the air and waved it.

Captain Maillard said, "As to the specific details of our counterattack, a decision has been made to withhold judgment in that area until we have reached actual rendezvous with the planet. Once we are in orbit and have a chance to study—" He paused and looked at Nolan's hand. "You have a question, young man?" He seemed genuinely surprised.

"At least one." Nolan looked at Carey when he spoke. "If these mines are so important—and I have no reason to doubt that they are—then wouldn't the simplest solution be to grant the demands of the workers and let them go back to work?"

Captain Maillard frowned. "I thought I had explained that these demands are both—"

"Yes, I know. Both unreasonable and treasonous. But you forgot one thing. What are they? Since this is what the rebellion is really about, I think we ought to know."

"I . . ." The captain looked at Carey, as if in need of help.

"I don't think that's any of your business, Lieutenant Nolan. The demands, if you must know, were made to my family's supervisors on Evron Eleven. They concern working conditions, living quarters, and other such matters. To put it bluntly, if granted, the demands would result in making the mines on Evron Eleven a totally unprofitable venture. They would have to be closed, which is exactly what we are ordered to prevent."

"Why? Couldn't they simply be sold? I'm not a rich man myself, but I'm far from convinced it's impossible to operate a business in a human manner without going broke."

"This is really rather irrelevant," Captain Maillard said.

"With all due respect, sir, I think you're mistaken," Nolan said. "To me, this entire mission, this vast boondoggle of a ship, with its crew of several hundred and us fifty or so corpsmen, is about to travel one hundred fifty-seven parsecs for no other reason that to protect the financial interests of one family. To me, that is what is really irrelevant. The

Empire and the Carey family are not identical commodities. I know that, and I suspect you do, too, Captain Maillard."

"I . . ." Captain Maillard began again. "I think you've said enough, lieutenant."

Carey said, "And I'd be glad to show Lieutenant Nolan—or anyone else who's interested—the order personally signed by Emperor Kane IV under which we will be proceeding."

Nolan was frowning. "I wasn't talking about the authority you've managed to grab, Carey. I was stating my personal opinion, and that was all."

"The lieutenant's opinion," Captain Maillard said, "verges upon the treasonous."

Nolan started to make another angry outburst, but Carey managed to cut him off. "Lieutenant Nolan's opinion is more uninformed than treasonous. You see, Lieutenant Nolan, since you chose to interrupt Captain Maillard before he could complete his briefing, there remains a fact of which you are unaware."

"What's that?" Nolan said. "That, if you lose your investment on Evron Eleven, you might have to start riding the slow shuttles with the rest of us?"

"No, not exactly," Carey said, with such obvious relish that Tedric sensed that whatever he was about to reveal was not only a surprise but an important surprise. "The unfortunate fact is, Lieutenant Nolan, that we are not the only ones to evidence an interest in the situation on Evron Eleven. Word has recently reached us that a large battle cruiser has gone into orbit around the world. I need not explain that a cruiser of such magnitude can have only one likely origin. A Wykzl fighting ship is operating inside the boundaries of the Empire of Man."

Nolan, along with everyone else, could only look stunned. No Wykzl ship had entered the Empire in the near century since the conclusion of the long war. If what Carey said was true, then it was not only a violation of treaty, it might also be a prelude to resumed armed conflict.

"But what can the Wykzl want with Evron Eleven?" Nolan asked, his surprise still showing.

"That," said Carey, his voice purring like a subman, "is what the Emperor has asked us to find out."

4 THE HIVES OF EVRON ELEVEN

One winter night at the Inn of the Four Crosses in South Lomarr, an old man in green robes stands before the assembled tavern guests and holds out both his hands. "As you can see," he says, "I have nothing concealed up my sleeves, nothing to hide from you. I'm a magician, not a trickster, but you must watch closely; watch closely please." The old man claps his hands once, twice, and there is a puff of blue smoke. Out of the smoke a tiny animal appears. It is a yellow bird.

The guests, more concerned with their drinks than the show, quietly applaud.

The magician bows.

At the back of the room in an unlighted corner, a lone man sits sipping ale. He does not applaud. He is huge, muscular, tall, and blond. He wears a longsword even here at the inn. His name, it is said, is Tedric. His occupation is that of ironmaster.

Tedric murmurs under his breath, "Ply your tricks now, old man, for in time they will mean nothing. In a world where magic does not exist, people can no longer be taken in by trickery."

With a mighty sweep of one hand, Tedric reaches out and wipes the table clear of glass and ale. His anger is beyond control. Four moons past, he reached the castle of Sarpedium only to find the black wizard gone. Now he searches for him everywhere, his sword constantly ready. Tedric observed horrors inside that dark castle that have transformed him from a man into an avenging angel.

He springs to his feet and shouts at the silent, stunned men around him: "I will kill all the wizards! I will kill them! I will!"

Tedric crunched his big frame into a tiny corner of the room he shared with Nolan and attempted with the aid of a metal file to hone a sharp point on his sword. A clock on the wall above his head told him that the common time aboard ship was presently 2325 hours.

The door opened. Tedric placed his sword over his knees and watched Phillip Nolan come stumbling through. It was easy to see from his bent spine, dangling arms, and grimy face that he had lately undergone another unendurable few hours of special duty.

Assistant Steward Third-Class Keller, who had been helping Tedric with his gear, jumped up from the floor and went to help Nolan inside.

"No, I can make it." Nolan waved Keller back

and stumbled unassisted toward the lower bunk. He rolled toward the berth, kicked his feet, and somehow made it safely into the tightly confined perch. He gave a sigh, snorted, rubbed his eyes, and finally said, "So we've finally arrived, I understand."

Keller, who continued to stand watch beside the bed, nodded. "At 1927 hours common ship time the *Eagleseye* entered normal space and is now orbiting the imperial planet, Evron Eleven."

"Thank the stars for that." Nolan shut his eyes. "Now perhaps I can get some rest."

"Is that what you want, Phillip?" Tedric, in his corner, had resumed work on the point of his sword.

"Do you know something I don't know?" Nolan asked, showing a degree of interest he had not previously evidenced. "I saw you walking around with Carey earlier on."

"We had a discussion." Tedric glanced at the tip of his sword and pressed the end of his thumb against it. He looked at the flesh, saw a drop of blood, and nodded. "I told him I felt what he was doing to you was not only wrong, it was a violation of the code of the Corps."

"And did he laugh then or later?"

"He didn't laugh at all."

Nolan frowned. He waved irritatedly at Keller, finally drove the subman away from his watch. "I never asked for your intervention, Tedric."

"Nor did I give it. Not really." He stood up, returned his sword to its sheath, and leaned it upright against the wall. Then he approached Nolan and rested his elbows against the edge of the upper bunk. "But I didn't believe your pride would stop short of achieving a decent night's rest."

"Perhaps not," said Nolan.

"And Carey agreed." What he was referring to was the strenuous duty schedule Nolan had been forced to endure ever since the moment, some thirty-two days back on the common calendar, when the *Eagleseye* had surpassed the velocity of light and entered the gray region of N-space. Since that time, Matthew Carey, as operations officer, had assigned Nolan to such tasks as scrubbing toilets, sweeping floors, polishing walls, and washing brass pots. Normally, such menial work was the strict province of the enlisted sailors, but Carey had not let either military tradition or official code stand in the way of his mistreatment of Nolan.

"You mean Carey has decided that he likes me after all." Nolan managed to chuckle past his exhaustion.

"Not exactly. But he has decided—"

"Hey, wait." Nolan sprang up, suddenly animate, and nearly cracked his head on the bunk above. "If we're in orbit, that means it ought to be possible to get a look at the Wykzl cruiser. Now that really is something worth seeing, a sight none of us is ever apt to get again."

But Tedric was frowning. "Keller and I already went down to the portholes to look. I'm afraid there's nothing to see, except for Evron Eleven itself, and it's a dull-looking world, brown and gray. The Wykzl ship is in orbit on the opposite side of the planet and the only way we'll ever get a close look is if one of us decides to chug up near and say hello."

"But it does exist? It wasn't just Carey's ploy?"

"No, it does exist. I went up to the bridge and read the printouts myself. There's something very big —and not a moon—in orbit back there."

Nolan dropped back down. "So much for new thrills in my life."

"But you didn't let Tedric finish what he was telling you, sir," Keller said.

"No, I guess I didn't. Tedric, I apologize. Please continue."

Tedric continued to lean against the top bunk. "I can tell you very simply, Phillip. Lieutenant Carey has named me to head a landing party which will be dropping down to the surface of Evron Eleven in approximately twelve hours."

"You?" Nolan said, with suspicion. "Why you?"

Tedric shrugged. "He said the reason was that I finished second in the class to him and thus deserved the second most responsible job. Personally, I think there are two reasons. One, he knows I'm a good fighter, and two, he wouldn't mind being rid of you for a short time."

"He's making me go with you?"

"He gave me free reign to pick my own landing party. Naturally, I selected you."

Nolan was wide awake now, as the dulling effects of his hours of tedious labor vanished. He lay propped on one elbow and scratched his cheek with a free hand. "You make me wonder why, Tedric."

"Oh, Phillip." Tedric moved away from the beds and crossed the room as well as he was able, side-stepping Keller. "Perhaps you're too suspicious for your own good. None of this is going to be easy. We're supposedly authorized to speak directly to the leaders of the rebellion, negotiate with them if we want, but basically—and Carey made this clear—we'll be going down there as spies. I don't think those workers will be fools. They'll know what we're up to, and they may simply decide to kill us. If I were them, I would, and I just have to hope they're more civilized than that."

"If they aren't, I doubt that Carey would mind."

Tedric nodded. "Exactly my feeling."

"A suicide mission?" Keller asked from the floor.

"Not unless that's what you feel like doing." Tedric picked up his sword and, for something to do, locked the belt around his waist. Lately, he had experienced a curious interest in the ancient weapon. The way it felt in his hands, the rock hard familiarity, was not a new sensation. He had felt it at the Academy, too, during fencing lessons, but it dated back much further than that. He had to wonder: was this another of the Scientists' buried memories rising to the surface, or could it be something deeper and rare, a lost recollection from that previous existence still known largely to him through the mists of his own dreams? There was no way of knowing, except waiting and letting experience reveal the truth.

"Be careful with that sword," Nolan warned jokingly. "The way you keep it sharp, you're apt to behead poor Keller some day."

"And we're going to need him, too," Tedric said.

"Keller's going with us?"

"We'll need someone to carry our stores and supplies. Keller has a good strong back and, besides, he knows something more of Evron Eleven that can be found out through tapes and recordings."

"I served a spell in the mines," Keller said softly. "It was before my entry into the navy. When they came and offered me a choice between the open spacelanes and those black pits, I never hesitated."

"How was it?" Nolan asked.

Keller shook his head. "Bad, sir, damned bad. I mean, the work was hard, sure, but so is this. They treat a person like an animal, like something lower than an animal. If the workers have finally rebelled, I say more power to them. Call me a traitor if you want and have me locked up, but I'm one man who knows the truth of what he speaks."

"No one here is going to call you a traitor, Keller," Nolan said.

"And Keller thinks he may still have friends on Evron Eleven. His wife remained behind."

"If she's not long since dead from overwork."

"Who else is going?" Nolan asked.

Tedric shook his head. "Do you have someone to recommend?"

Nolan thought for a moment, then said no. "Not anyone in particular, no. We're all evenly experienced, which is to say that we have no real experience. There are some good men in the class, but no one who really stands out above the rest."

"I felt that way, too."

"And you chose?"

"No one. The three of us. The way I see it, if we're going to be spies, we ought to do it right. A party of ten or twenty tramping through the mines won't make us exactly inconspicuous."

"You, me, and Keller," Nolan said thoughtfully. "It's like the three musketeers."

"Who?" asked Tedric, confused.

"Oh, some famous men who lived once long ago. All for one and one for all. That was their credo."

"What does it mean?"

Nolan laughed, shaking his head. "You know, I've never quite figured that out, either." He turned on his side and faced the wall. "Now let us sleep," he murmured past a broad yawn.

And Tedric let him.

The savage thrust of acceleration five times greater than normal Earth gravity slammed Tedric hard against the soft cushion of the horizontal couch in which he rode. He struggled to make his spine less rigid, tried to force his muscles to relax and flow like liquid into the pliant surface beneath. Outside, through the tiny round porthole, he could see the sky ablaze with a crimson flash.

We could be dying, he thought. There's no way a man can endure this force.

But he knew from his studies in history, if nothing else, that men had endured this same force since the dawn of the age of space. Few simpler methods had yet been devised for reaching the surface of a planet than a parachute drop.

Nolan and Keller, who had both done this before, nevertheless showed the pain of their five-G ordeal. Their mouths hung open, their faces distorted with the force, their brows were covered with perspiration. But we will live, Tedric decided. This is not just a way of making us die.

Then the parachute unfurled and caught, and Tedric was thrown forward against the straps of his couch. The sky outside turned in an instant from blazing red to pitch black, and he knew as he struggled to catch enough air to breathe that the capsule was now floating gently downward through the midnight dark of Evron Eleven toward the as yet unseen surface below. Tedric finally found a word he could make his tongue utter aloud. "Whew," he said, with true feeling.

Nolan, strapped to the couch to Tedric's right, turned his head and managed a weak grin. "We dropped harder than I expected. There was a minute when I think I actually blacked out, and that should never happen."

"Do you think it's because the planet has a mass

greater than its volume would normally indicate, an abnormally high density?" Tedric spoke from the lessons he had learned at the Imperial Academy, but the knowledge never quite seemed to be a part of him. It was something extraneous, like a suit of borrowed clothes.

"That's possible," Nolan said, "but I'd rather blame Carey. I think he wanted to make our trip as uncomfortable as possible."

"He has no authority over a capsule launch."

"He has authority wherever he chooses to exercise it. Who do you think is going to step forward and tell him he's wrong? Not dear Captain Maillard, that's for sure."

Tedric said nothing. Because of the way Nolan had been treated during the course of the voyage, his obsessive dislike of Carey had, if anything, increased. Tedric knew there was little point in trying to argue rationally about the matter.

All three men knew better than to unfasten their straps quite yet. The final impact of actual landing still awaited them.

Tedric turned his head and saw through the porthole the familiar pattern of Evron Eleven's nighttime stars. He had memorized the local starmap as a prelude to finding his way around this strange planet.

Unless another miscalculation had occurred, the capsule ought to set down some ten kilometers northwest of the present headquarters of the rebellious workers. Despite its planetary character, Evron

Eleven was only sporadically inhabited. The mining of Dalkanium had begun on the planet less than a century ago, and so far only a few especially rich lodes were being followed. The rebellion had largely been limited to the site of the largest mine, where approximately one thousand workers presently held fewer than fifty supervisors and corporate officials prisoner. Because of this, the rebellion might possibly be contained with some ease, and it was for this reason—he claimed—that Carey had decided to begin his counterattack with a small landing party.

"I wish I could have brought my dulcetone," Keller said. "If there was ever a time when a song would go good, it's now, when you're floating through the air with nothing on your mind."

"I didn't know you were a musician," Nolan said, and Tedric was glad of the diversion to draw Nolan's thoughts away from Matthew Carey.

"In my time, I've been a little bit of everything," Keller said. "I'm more a singer than a musician, though."

"Then why don't you sing?" Tedric said. "We're good listeners."

"Got any favorites?"

"No, not especially." It took a question like that to make Tedric realize there wasn't a single song he could honestly say that he knew. Or was that true? A faint tune hummed at the back of his mind, but it stayed there, not quite audible. Another memory? From how far back?

"Then I'll try this one on you." Keller broke into a song that concerned a beautiful maiden from a planet named Glencora whose loving man had gone to fight the war. Despite a happy, soaring melody, the song was almost a lament, as the maiden cried for her lover's return and saw him again only when he was brought back from the farthest reaches of space, as dead as a stone. Then she wept over his grave until her tears alone caused his soul to swell out and speak of its love before it fell back and she died and a flower grew where she lay.

Nolan was frowning. "I hardly think that's what we need to hear now."

"It always cheers me up," Keller said, with the hint of a grin.

"If you're partial to graves and ghosts and dead women, I suppose so."

"I enjoyed it very much," Tedric said, but again a memory was stirring. What was it this time? Was it the music again?

Before he could make any serious effort to answer these questions, there was a sudden jolt. Tedric bounced against the straps that held him to the couch, then bounced again and lay still.

"We're here," Nolan said.

Keller was the first one free of his couch and he hurried to help Nolan and Tedric.

When he could, Tedric stood up and went over to the porthole. Evron Eleven was a moonless world and there was only starlight with which to see. The landscape appeared to be a barren stretch, littered with a few large boulders and rocks.

He turned away from the port. "We'd better get out of here and try to conceal the capsule. Someone may have seen the flash of our descent."

"I doubt that." Nolan shrugged quickly into his necessary gear: holster, belt, heatgun, sword. "Not unless we've missed our mark. The mine ought to be well past the horizon."

"And it is underground," Keller added. He was drawing together the backpacks each would have to wear.

"Still, we can't be sure. Maybe someone was outside, watching the stars."

"A pair of Keller's doom-struck lovers," Nolan said.

But Keller shook his head. "Nobody ever falls in love on Evron Eleven."

It required only a few additional moments before the men were properly outfitted and ready to venture out. Tedric punched the button that controlled the lock and was the first to look through the opening.

The air was sharp, heavy in oxygen, and a chill wind seemed to be blowing. He blinked several times to acquaint his eyes with the darkness, then leaped to the ground. The earth was soft and malleable, a fine but moist dust that stuck to the soles of his boots. He ignited the battery flash he wore at his waist and turned in a complete circle, surveying the landscape. His first impression proved accurate. Rocks and boulders, little else. In the distance, there stood a twisted outline that might have been a leafless tree.

He waved back at Nolan and Keller. "It seems safe. Let's get going."

Nolan came first, then Keller, who turned before making his leap and set the lock to close behind them.

"There's no way we can attempt to conceal the capsule here," Nolan said. "It's too big to snuggle under the edge of a rock."

"I'll set the directional beam and then we'll just have to hope it's still here when we come back."

"If we do come back."

"And, don't forget, we can always radio the *Eagleseye* for help. It's not as if we're totally alone." Of course, it wasn't safe to use their radios now. Tedric had broken off communication with the *Eagleseye* as soon as their capsule penetrated the upper atmosphere. Although their orders had left the question open, Tedric and Nolan had earlier decided not to attempt to contact the rebel leaders openly, at least not until after an initial, secretive survey of the situation. Any radio contact with the *Eagleseye* ran the risk of drawing attention to their presence on the surface, and that was what they presently wished to avoid above all else. Nolan had hinted that Carey might possibly have sent them down knowing in advance the rebels would surely kill them if they caught them. While Tedric couldn't bring himself to accept such a devious premise, he still intended to exercise some care.

Tedric removed the directional beacon from a pouch on his belt and handed it to Keller to bury in the loose dust at the bottom of the capsule. The beam given off by the beacon would lock on the *Eagleseye* alone. If nothing else, it would serve as an indication of their safe arrival.

When Keller finished, Tedric motioned him and Nolan away from the capsule and, pointing the beam of his flash ahead, started off in the direction of the mines. It would be a considerable hike, even if the land remained flat and relatively clear, and they could not hope to reach their destination much before noon the next day.

None of them spoke. There was a certain alienness about this world that seemed to affect even Keller, who had once lived there. There was the silence, too—the utter stillness and absence of life. The grotesque hulks of the bigger boulders loomed on all sides, casting crazy shadows when the beam of the flash washed across them.

When the men came out of ambush, there was no warning whatsoever. Tedric saw them before the others and shouted. He reached for his sword and drew it swiftly. Only later did he realize that a heatgun would have served better than a sword, but he was only able to react instinctively. He didn't count the men who came at him. They had hidden behind a broad collection of boulders, and there might have been as many as twenty.

The nearest man showed clearly in the beam of

the flash. He was short, squat, and hairy, more like an animal than a man. Tedric kept this impression as he rushed forward to meet his attacker. He threw back his sword and swung from his hips. The blade made a whistling noise as it rushed through the air. The man screamed once, suddenly aware of the danger, before the blade struck his neck. His head tilted to one side, nearly severed, and he toppled in a gush of pumping blood.

Tedric fell back, astonished at what he had done. I've just killed a human being, he thought, a man I never knew in my life. He felt disgusted, excited, and stunned. For a moment, he couldn't move at all.

And, in that brief interval, the others were upon him.

As he grappled with his attackers, he had time to see Keller and Nolan, both pinned underneath a half-dozen men. Tedric strained to break loose from the men who held him. He wanted to use his sword, but someone had hold of his hands. His head was drawn back. There were rigid fingers at his throat.

Then he heard someone shout: "Don't kill them! Be careful! You know we want them alive!"

The voice puzzled him. It sounded too shrill, almost inhuman.

Then he realized what it must mean: the person who had shouted was someone he had never seen in this universe before.

It was a woman.

Then he did see her. Only briefly. She stood high

on a boulder, her hands waving furiously as she directed her men. He felt a momentary sense of impotency. He knew he was beaten and knew a woman had led the attack.

But then he decided to struggle back. In a sudden swift move, he twisted his body and stretched his muscles to the breaking point. He swung his arms and managed to break free of the men who held his arms. He turned his sword and prepared to cut.

But then someone hit him with a rock. He knew as soon as he felt the blow what it must be. An instant later, the pain overwhelmed him. He staggered and nearly dropped to his knees.

The rock hit him again. Not as hard as before, but hard.

He fell. His lips tasted the moist dust of Evron Eleven. And, just an instant before he lost consciousness completely, he managed to turn his head slightly and gaze upward.

His conqueror stood there, rock in hand, and despite the faint starlight, he could see who it was. A woman. Another woman.

And, just then, before the blackness consumed him, he realized what else was true. Even the one he had killed. She had been a woman, too.

Tedric awoke the first time with his skull on fire and tried to grab hold of his throbbing head.

He couldn't. His hands were tied.

He opened his eyes and discovered the source of

the throbbing. He was being carried on a wooden post, his hands and legs wrapped around the body of the wood. His bearers, two figures he could see only dimly in the corners of his vision, made no effort to give him a gentle ride. The post bumped each time they took a step.

He could see nothing else. Not Nolan. Not Keller. There was nothing in his world but the pain in his head and the discomfort of his perch.

He shut his eyes. He would sleep again. There was no reason for wakefulness now, no reason for thought.

When Tedric awoke the second time, he sat on a cold, smooth floor. His arms were still tied, and so were his legs. A blinding white light as bright as a sun tore at his eyes. He shut them and felt the persistent pounding in his head. He decided to try his eyes again and this time discovered the source of the light was nothing more than a flickering lantern.

The room where he sat, his spine propped against a wall, was underground and cramped. Even free, there would barely have been room to move. He saw Keller seated to his right, securely bound, and Nolan to his left. Only Keller was awake.

Tedric licked his lips, then tried to speak. His tongue felt swollen but the words seemed comprehensible. "So we are alive?"

Keller nodded. "I am at least, and so's Nolan. He was awake a few minutes ago. We were worried about you, though."

"Someone hit me on the head with a rock."

"I know. I saw it. You sure fought like the devil against them. I wanted to, but they were on me before I half-knew what was happening. I'm sorry. You could have used the help."

Tedric frowned. "No matter. There were too many of them for us to handle."

"Women, too. I should have known. They out-number the men twenty to one in the mines. That's because they're sold by their parents."

"Sold? Like slaves?"

"Contracted I think is the word they prefer to use."

Tedric frowned. "But they knew exactly where we were. That's what I don't like. It was almost as if they were waiting for us."

The sound of voices must have roused Nolan from his sleep. "I see you've come to the same conclu-sion I did. It must have been Carey. Damn him. He sent us down here to die and then called the gravedig-gers personally."

"We don't know that for sure."

"We do unless we're hopelessly stupid."

Tedric shrugged as well as his ropes would allow. He didn't want to get into an argument with Nolan, not when he thought what Nolan was saying most likely was true. He asked Keller, "Can you guess where we are?"

"In the mines, that's for sure, but exactly where, I can't say. Some of the shafts plunge far underground to follow a particular lode. Some parts of Evron

Eleven are like hives. The workers are drones. They go for years without seeing the sun."

"But have you seen any of them since we came here?"

Keller shook his head. "Not a soul."

"And maybe that's just how it'll stay," said Nolan. "What could be easier? They bring us down here, tons of rock over our heads, and leave us to rot."

Tedric shook his head. "Then why bother? They could have killed us just as easily when they first caught us."

But Nolan shook his head, unpersuaded by logic, and when what seemed like many additional hours had passed without anyone coming to see them, Tedric began to wonder himself. He slept, he woke, he slept again. Sometimes he and Keller exchanged a few words. Less frequently, Nolan joined them.

But at last, as Tedric had anticipated must happen, the wooden door that separated their cell from whatever lay beyond creaked on its hinges and slid open.

The figure of a woman came through. She was very tall, very thin, with a round face and yellow fur. A subman—or subwoman. Tedric could not be sure if this was the same woman who had led the ambush.

But Keller seemed to know her. His eyes grew wide with recognition and he cried out: "Jania—it's you!"

The woman frowned with contempt. "Who told you my name?"

"No one had to tell me. Don't you know? I'm Keller—I'm your husband."

The woman—Jania—shook her head. "My husband died many years ago."

"But I'm him!"

She shrugged, dismissing Keller's claims without another thought, and came over and stood in front of Tedric. "You wear the insignia of an officer in the Corps. I want you to answer my questions to the best of your knowledge."

Tedric shook his head. It was hard taking this woman at all seriously. "I can only speak to the rebel leaders."

Jania laughed. "I am their leader."

"You?" said Tedric.

"Me." She sat down across from him, still laughing. "This is Evron Eleven, not one of your party planets. We don't have time to worry about proper roles. I have to work in the mines as hard as any man. I can lead them, too."

"I wasn't disputing your abilities," Tedric said.

"Then perhaps you won't mind answering my questions either."

5 RATS IN THE PITS

The High Priestess of Acadium, who is said to see the far future with the clarity of the present moment, resides in a mud hut on Jayne Isle at the center of Lake Nohowan in North Lomarr. Few ever dare venture there, for the Priestess is known to be as whimsical as she is powerful and ready to kill a man as easily as she might please him.

Tedric approaches the mud hut without hesitation and bangs on the wooden door with the hilt of his sword. "Open, up, old woman. I, Tedric, Lord of the Marshes, have come to discover the whereabouts of Sarpedium, the black wizard."

A crone with swollen black eyes opens the door. She squints at Tedric, then cackles in glee. "But you are Tedric, the man of science not magic. You have no use for my powers. Go away and find the wizard yourself. Go or you will die in your footsteps."

Tedric reaches out before the crone can close the door. He grips her bony throat and says, "You will serve me, old fool, or you will die."

"Your sword holds no power here," she gasps.
"Will you try it?" He senses the fear beneath her scorn.
"Release me."
"When you have served me."
"I cannot serve you here."
Tedric lets her go. The hut, inside, reeks of foul fumes.
The Priestess mixes her bitter brew and drinks deeply of the
potion. She falls to the floor and squirms. Tedric clutches
her shoulders.
The Priestess chants: Sarpedium . . . black wizard . . .
I see a cold, cunning, cruel face . . . he stands among youth
. . . women . . . lovely maidens . . . they dance . . . he—"
Tedric slaps her. "No riddles. The truth, fool. I want it
now. Where is Sarpedium?"
But he will learn no more from her. Magic works only
through riddles. Tedric must learn that, too.

The traincar in which they rode crawled along
the underground rails at a velocity of less than five
kilometers per hour.

But that was deliberate.

Their guide, Jania, wanted them to see, and for
that, haste would serve no useful purpose.

Tedric himself, as patient as could be, had remained content all day simply to watch and observe.
Now, as the traincar plunged downward toward the
deepest pits, his ears kept plugging. Tedric coughed
and swallowed to clear the passages. Behind, in the
rear, Nolan and Keller did the same. Jania seemed
unaffected by the rigors of their descent. She had
spent at least a dozen years in the mines, if she was

indeed Keller's wife as he continued to claim, and had only infrequently glimpsed the light of day in that time. The four of them rode alone. There were no guards, and Jania carried nothing deadlier than a slim, handmade dagger that looked too brittle to kill. There was no escape down here for anyone. In the past few hours, Tedric had seen enough to convince him of that.

The idea of this tour was Jania's own. When she had first come to get them, the women with her (and a lone man) had argued vehemently in opposition. Jania had won out, the force of her personality more than sufficient to carry her side. Tedric thought, if he wanted to break the spine of the rebellion, he knew exactly where to begin: with Jania. Already, in one short day among the rebels, he had seen enough to convince him that she alone among them was a natural leader. But did he want to break the rebellion? What he had seen and learned today had made that suddenly an open question.

Jania touched the handbrake and the traincar slowed to a stop. She reached past Tedric and pointed outside. "Here, we're stopping. This is something else I think you should see."

"Not more," said Nolan bleakly, from his place in the back seat. His voice resembled that of a beaten man. "Haven't we endured enough horrors to suit you?"

"You haven't endured them," Jania said. "You've seen them. That's not the same."

Tedric understood what she meant, but he also

sympathized with Nolan's fatigue. Keller was the only one who had remained untouched by what Jania had shown them, but Keller had lived here before, and Tedric doubted very much had changed in the interim.

Jania touched a dashboard control that ignited a faint light on the outside of the car. "Now look and tell me if that's enough," she said.

With the others, Tedric tried to look, but a thick mist, almost a fog, hugged the bottom of the cavern and rose here and there in thick swirls. Jania touched another control, and then they could hear: the sharp, steady beat of picks and shovels. Tedric stared and finally made out through the mist a small, moving figure. Then there was another. And a third. One stepped out of the mist, pushing a wheelbarrow in front of him, and moved alongside the traincar for a brief moment. He—although, in truth, it was most likely a girl—seemed unaware of their presence. Tedric listened to the creaking wheels of the barrow as it disappeared in the distance.

"They're children," Nolan finally said.

"Yes, and do you know why?" Jania asked.

"No, not exactly. I'm not . . . not surprised, though," Tedric agreed. After some of the things he had seen today, he doubted that anything would ever surprise him again.

"Guess," Jania said.

"It's because of the gas," Keller said. He spoke softly, recalling the facts from long-buried memories. "It kills them."

"Exactly," she said. "It kills them."

"You don't mean that white stuff, that mist?" Tedric said.

"It's a gas sealed deep beneath the planetary surface and released by the digging. It doesn't kill at once. Don't misunderstand me. If you or I went out there and walked around, we'd get sick but we wouldn't die. The children seldom get sick. They simply die."

Tedric watched the ghostly figures of the children as they drifted through the pale cloud of deadly mist. "Then why is it necessary to use children?"

"For the same reason anyone is used here. We're submen, subwomen, and thus not quite human. We're expendable, and the children are even more expendable than the rest of us. If you have to lose a worker, it might as well be one too young to carry a proper load."

"Children grow up," Nolan said.

"Not here. Not in these pits. I've stayed alive for twelve years and I'm considered a freak, a rarity among rarities."

"Then why not protect them some way? The gas leak could be sealed up. Oxygen masks could be provided."

"That's all been tried. Years and years ago when the operation began here. The leaks can't be sealed because that would mean sealing up the Dalkanium that's in there, too, and Dalkanium mining is, after all, our only business here. As far as protective masks are concerned, that's been tried, too, and it hasn't worked. They slip, they come loose, people forget to wear them. Have you ever tried to force a child to wear something like that for hours at a time?"

"Then don't use children."

"I've already explained to you why that isn't done."

"It's murder," Nolan finally said, giving up his argument.

"That's what I've been trying to show you."

Jania released the brake, and the traincar rolled on.

It had been the same all day—one scene following another with no apparent end. Tedric felt numb. Worse than numb. He felt sickened.

"Oh, I could show you more," Jania said, as she drove. "I could have brought you close and let you see the faces on those children. Some you would have sworn couldn't be younger than eighty. But it's all the same. It's all terrible. And yet you come here and tell us we're wrong to rebel. You tell us to go back to work for the good of the Empire."

"I never told you that," Nolan said.

"But you believe it."

"No, not me. Never."

Jania laughed. The traincar wheeled around a sudden sharp corner, then dropped with unexpected velocity. "This will be the last of it," she said. "One more thing to see, and then we'll head back up. This is the bottom shaft. This is what it's taken a century to reach. I thought you'd be interested in seeing what so much suffering has finally accomplished."

Tedric nodded, gripping the edge of his seat tightly to keep from tumbling forward. The day had begun with a brief private meeting with the corporation supervisors held hostage by the rebels. The men —none were women—seemed no worse off for their captivity. They were healthy, well-fed, and—this was the impression Tedric received most strongly—thoroughly confused by what had happened. As the day progressed and he saw more and more of the true reality of the mines, he couldn't help wondering if these apparently decent men had any accurate conception of what went on under their authority. Jania explained that the supervisors themselves seldom ventured far into the mine shafts. They set annual quotas and daily allotments but left the actual responsibility for meeting these up to the miners themselves and a handful of trustee foremen chosen from the ranks of the workers.

"And where are these foremen?" Tedric asked. "Did they join your rebellion or are they prisoners, too?"

"They're neither," Jania said softly. "They're dead."

Cold-blooded murder, whatever its motive, disturbed him, but so did the economics of the situation, and he had soon come to understand, during the course of Jania's tour, why Nolan called it slavery. The workers were paid a set wage, it was true, but no money exchanged hands. Instead, a paper sum was recorded each year and from this amount food, lodging, clothes, tools, and transportation were deducted.

At the end of the first year, a worker might have a considerable sum credited to his name, but it was never sufficient to pay for the price of return passage, and it never would be. Jania had shown them her own calculations, which indicated that, with the high cost of injuries and accidents, a worker would have to spend at least twenty years in the mines to build up enough credit to pay for a trip to the nearest inhabited world, and no worker ever lived that long. Tedric asked Jania if she knew of one person who had succeeded in leaving Evron Eleven alive, and she said the only examples she knew were a few males who had volunteered to serve in the navy and earned their freedom that way. For a woman, there was no way out, and for that reason—as well as what she called feminine endurance—the percentage of women in the mines continued to rise.

There was also the question of the Dalkanium itself. Jania believed that the element was sufficiently active in its raw form to receive the blame for much of the physical ills of the miners.

"If a landslide doesn't get you," she said, "or a cave-in, a gas leak or a vicious foreman with a whip, then the Dalkanium itself is a slow death of its own."

Tedric had spoken to workers who seemed to be seventy and eighty years of age. Jania swore there was no one in the mines much past thirty.

The traincar was moving faster now. Even in this absolute darkness, Tedric sensed the walls of the tunnel flashing past.

He had seen no reason in raising the subject himself, but Nolan apparently preferred a more direct attack. "If this is the end of our tour," he asked Jania, "then what's going to happen to us now?"

Tedric heard Jania chuckling softly. "What do you expect?"

She had revealed at the beginning of the tour how she and the other rebels had learned of their presence on the surface of Evron Eleven. It was as Nolan had guessed: a message picked up from the orbiting *Eagleseye* had given away their probable landing site. But the message was not aimed at the rebels. Its interception might have been an unforeseen accident. Tedric was not ready to blame Carey quite so soon.

"Then who was he calling?" Nolan had asked "He had to be trying to alert the rebels. There's nobody else here but us."

"Have you forgotten the Wykzl ship so soon?" Tedric asked.

"But why would Carey be telling them about us?"

Tedric had not been able to answer that question. But it was something worth thinking about, an intimation of a far more complex situation than any of them might yet be aware.

Jania, still chuckling, attempted to answer Nolan's question regarding their possible future fate. "To tell you the truth, I haven't made a final decision. I'll say one thing, though. The majority of us don't favor having you killed."

"Well, that only makes sense," Nolan said. "We could help you, Jania, argue your case in places where it matters."

"No." She laughed without humor. "Don't try to fool me with false promises. No one can help us, not even ourselves."

"Then what do you intend doing with us?" Tedric saw no reason to keep silent now that Nolan had raised the matter.

"Most likely, we'll do nothing more to you than what you've already done to us. We'll put you to work —you and the other supervisors. We'll let you have a taste of the life you've forced us to endure."

"You can't blame us," Nolan said. "My family has historically opposed mercenary labor systems. It's the Careys you ought to be after."

"We don't have them. We have you."

"But that's not fair."

"Neither is this," she said, waving a hand at the nearby walls flashing past.

For Tedric, the most puzzling thing he had seen here in the mines was the way the workers continued to go about their regular tasks in spite of the success of their rebellion. He had asked Jania about this and she had said that most at first had indeed quit.

"But then they found themselves with time on their hands," she said, "and down here, what can you do? Eat? Sleep? That grows boring after a while. Read books? Watch videos? Most of us don't have the eyes for that anymore. Sit and wait and hope that we might be saved? No, we couldn't just do that. So we went back to work. It happened slowly at first. One person, then another, until now, as you can see, nearly everyone is working again. Before you came, I was lifting a pick myself. I hated it, I loathed myself, but what else could I do?"

For Tedric, her explanation was perhaps the most horrible thing of all.

The traincar was slowing now. Tedric relaxed his grip on the seat and leaned slowly back against the cushion rest. He heard the gentle whining of brakes and saw Jania's hand pumping fitfully in the dark. The car ended its descent and moved on a flat plane. Then it stopped.

"Here," Jania said. "This is it—the end. Come on, you'll have to go out to see this."

"Won't we require protective gear?" Nolan asked.

"You mean because of the Dalkanium? Oh, no. You'll live. Don't worry. That's the least thing you have to fear."

Reaching forward, she touched a lever that simultaneously ignited a small outside searchlight and caused the roof of the car to roll back. Jania leaped over the side, and Tedric joined her. Nolan and Keller came, too, if more hesitantly. In the circle of illumination given off by the light, there was nothing to see but the rock walls and floor of the narrow tunnel. Still, distantly, Tedric heard the by now familiar rhythm of falling picks and shovels.

He noted also that the rails ended here. Jania was right. This was indeed the end of her world.

"We'll go this way." Jania turned on a small hand flashlight and led them down the length of the tunnel. The roof seemed very close overhead and, as they proceeded, it came even closer. It seemed cold down here, too. The air was thin and damp. Nolan shivered and rubbed at his arms. His teeth chattered wildly.

Then someone screamed.

The four of them stopped. Tedric listened and heard, in the surrounding darkness, the scampering of tiny feet. It sounded more like an animal than anything even remotely human.

"Be careful," Jania said. "They won't hurt us but they can be frightened."

"Who's they?" Nolan asked.

"You'll see—soon enough." She started off once again, and they followed. The tunnel continued to slope toward a point like the tapered blade of a longsword.

Keller said, "I don't remember this part, Jania."

"No, you wouldn't—not unless you had worked down here, and that was never possible. Only a few of the supervisors knew about this before the rebellion. We only found out later." Tedric thought this was as close as Jania had yet come to acknowledging Keller as her husband.

As the tunnel sloped even further, Tedric ducked his head and bent his knees. With Jania leading, their steps came slowly, as if no one was eager to reach the end. Jania pointed her light at the rising floor. Tedric saw occasional bright flecks flashing among the dark rocks. The Dalkanium, he assumed. It glowed here and there throughout the black cavern like the peering eyes of tiny motionless insects.

The noise of the workers ahead grew increasingly louder.

Jania stopped. She was breathing heavily. Because of the thin air? Or something else? "I'm going to have to dim the light. Don't be startled."

"No, go ahead." Tedric felt like a huntsman stalking unseen prey. But what could it be? he wondered. The noise of shovels and picks made it seem merely human. But that didn't explain his anxiety, his sense that something was very wrong indeed. They moved forward again. Did Tedric really want to reach the end?

The noise stopped suddenly. *Ping, ping, ping,* then silence. They hear us, thought Tedric. They know we're coming.

But who? Or, what?

"Hush," Jania whispered. "Don't speak one more word. Not a sound. Or a whisper."

She took a step. Another. Tedric followed. Then Nolan. Keller. She took a step. Another.

The tunnel turned a sudden corner and there, on the opposite side, the roof dropped abruptly, the sides closed in, and the floor rose. Jania crouched down. Tedric peered past her shoulder. Their bodies blocked the passage.

Jania turned her light ahead.

They saw it.

Tedric gasped. Nolan stiffled a cry. Keller murmured, "Oh, no. Oh, no."

"Hush. If you can," Jania whispered. "Just look. Don't move or talk. They're easily frightened."

At the very end of the tunnel—the point of the sword—five of them stood. Five . . . what? Men? Women? Children?

Five creatures—five vaguely human beings.

None stood higher than a meter from the ground. Their trunks were the size of a normal man, but their legs and feet were shrunken to the point where they barely seemed to exist. And their hands—huge, clutching paws—dangled from the slender wrists of arms longer than their bodies.

And the eyes. The eyes were like huge, gaping black pits.

"They're blind," Tedric said, with a note of pity in his voice.

Jania laughed softly. "No, they can see you all right. Not with their eyes, but they can see."

"They're not human."

"They are."

"Not like you and I. Not men, not submen."

"Exactly the same."

The five creatures seemed disturbed, frightened. They waddled to and fro across the beam of Jania's light. And they cried out. Shrill, frail, piercing cries.

Jania lowered the light until all they could see were shadows.

"That—that can't exist," said Nolan.

"But it does." Her voice was strong, positive. "You saw it and I saw it. Are we to call our own eyes liars?"

"But—but how? And why?"

"How? Through the workings of the genera-tions. Son after son after son buried in these deepest pits. A hundred years of sons—or daughters—with none living more than a dozen years. I know how it happened, but I don't know why. These are our real leaders. These are physical representations of what we all will become someday."

Shielded from the light which had frightened them, the creatures had resumed their work. One clasped a pick in his huge hands and struck at the face of the rock. Another slapped at the broken stones with the butt of his shovel. The other three used their bare hands, tearing at the rock with an intensity no flesh could bear. And they continued to cry out, their shrill howls rising like a madman's joyous song.

Tedric thought of an animal he had never seen, only read about. It had originated on Earth and spread quickly throughout the Empire of Man.

Tedric thought of the rat. That is what these poor things were: rats in the pits. Children of the mines.

The rumbling of the earth caught them all by surprise. It began like the pounding of a giant's foot-steps far in the distance but then grew closer. And louder. The rock at their feet began to tremble.

"Cave-in," Jania said softly. "Something's falling somewhere."

"But are we safe?"

Jania stretched out her arms and grabbed hold of both shaking walls as if to keep them from collapsing inward. "We won't know till it's over."

"When will it be over?"

"Shut up."

They waited. The rumbling grew briefly more intense, hit a peak, then slowly subsided. Not until it was over and their tiny world still again did Tedric realize that the entire sequence of events had taken less than a minute to complete.

As soon as the rumbling ceased, Jania was off and running. Keeping his head close to his chest until the tunnel allowed him enough room to stand upright, Tedric ran after her. The four of them reached the traincar at the same time. From behind, the noise of falling picks and shovels went on. The creatures had never stopped. Throughout the quake, they had continued to dig, oblivious to the existence of any world outside their own.

They climbed into the traincar. Jania lowered the roof, then started the electric engine. The car zoomed off along the tracks, moving in reverse now, retracing their past trail. Tedric thought about what might lie ahead, but he knew he would never forget what he had seen behind.

The traincar began to climb. Tedric, glancing past his shoulder to see ahead, noticed a thickness in the air. Jania confirmed his impression. "Dust. From the cave-in."

"Then it's close?"

"Or else damned big."

The traincar reached the end of its high ascent, then climbed more gradually. Tedric thought he recognized the spot where they had first paused to watch the children at work among the thick gas. The car hurried past that point and went on.

"It may not have affected us at all," Nolan said. "The tunnels down here are like a thicket in a maze. If one passage is blocked, there's always another."

"Not this near the bottom," Jania said. "Down here, there's just one way out. Unless . . ."

"Yes?" said Nolan, clearly willing to clutch at any possible excuse for optimism.

"Unless we can break free of this main tunnel and reach the first branch."

"And how far is that from here?"

"Another hundred meters. No more."

"Then we might—"

But Nolan stopped. The traincar had swerved around a sharp corner. Jania jammed on the brakes. The dust here was as thick as a blanket of fog.

Without a word, Jania edged the car slowly forward. They went ten meters, perhaps fifteen, when she stopped again. Reaching out, she turned the outside light to its highest intensity.

What lay ahead was plain to see. The dust, as thick as it was, failed to conceal the truth.

A wall of solid rock blocked their way.

6 PREMATURE BURIAL

The raft that crosses the River Bolla between the towns of Crux and Novale is crowded this night. Among those seated on deck is an old beggar dressed in torn burlap who clutches a long parcel wrapped in soiled cloth.

From a distance, the beggar appears to be asleep, his chin lolling upon his chest. But he is listening. Nearby, a nomadic trader is describing to a companion a strange sight he has recently seen.

The trader says, "At first I assumed it must be an inn or tavern, and since I was very tired, I decided to stop and see if I might find lodgings for the night. The house was very bright, with every window well lighted, so I knocked at the door and a young woman answered. She was lean, beautiful, and meagerly dressed, so then I assumed the place must be a bawdy house. I asked after a room, and the woman smiled shyly and stepped back as if to let me pass."

"And did you actually go inside?" asks his friend.

"I began to," the trader says, "until I noticed some-

thing that disturbed me. This was glowing." He indicates a silver talisman around his throat. "*It was given to my grandfather as a protection against evil. I had never known it to glow that way before.*"

"*And then you ran away?*"

"*Then I stopped. No, it was what happened next that caused me to flee. I had come far enough inside to see beyond the door. There were more women, at least a dozen, all as beautiful as the first. Then I heard the scream. It came from above and was clearly that of a man. I have heard nothing so terrible in my life. It was the scream of a man imprisoned in hell and unable to escape. It went on and on, without end. Then I ran.*"

"*And these women made no effort to prevent you?*"

"*Oh, they tried. They tore at my garments with fingers like claws. I still bear the scars of several of my wounds. Still, the talisman seemed to frighten them. I think it saved my life. But it was not them I most feared. It was whatever lay above, upstairs. I could sense its presence the whole time —a dark, dank, filthy, horrible thing. I don't know what it was.*"

"*Excuse me.*" The beggar, suddenly awake, leans close. "*Could you please tell me exactly where to find this house?*"

"*You? You?*" The trader laughs in a burst. "*Why would you ever want to know that?*"

"*Because I intend to go there,*" says Lord Tedric of the Marshes, "*and kill the dark, dank, horrible thing you have described.*"

"*You know what it is?*"

"*Sarpedium, the black wizard of death.*"

Jania dropped stiffly back in the seat. She raised her hands, placed them against her cheeks, and drew the fingers slowly down the ridges of her face. It was the only outward indication of emotion she gave. She neither lamented nor raged.

Tedric pointed at the dashboard. "I think we ought to use the radio."

"Through this mountain of rock?" She lifted a hand toward the obstruction ahead.

"We're going to need help to get out of here."

"Yes. I suppose you're right." She shrugged. "All right, I'll try."

"Go ahead."

In the back, Nolan and Keller seemed too stunned to speak. Tedric was glad of that. He and Jania were having enough trouble keeping their own emotions from showing. The addition of two more frightened voices would help no one.

Jania concentrated on the dashboard controls. She turned dials and adjusted levers. There was a shrill whistling noise, like steam escaping a kettle, then a burst of static.

And finally a voice—a whisper—barely audible.

Jania turned up the volume control. "This is Jania speaking. Can anyone hear me? Answer if you can. This is an emergency."

"Jania." The voice now came with startling clarity.

"Is that you, Carla?" Her tone remained deliberately cool.

"Yes, it's me—it's Carla. Jania, then it is you. We all thought—we'd assumed you were dead."

"There was an accident. A cave-in. The prisoners are with me and fine. Now listen. Listen carefully. We are located on level fourteen of the lower tunnel, approximately three hundred fifty meters above gas leak seven. The tunnel ahead is apparently blocked completely. What we need is help from your side. Any help. Anyone who can dig us out."

"Jania, we don't . . ." The voice seemed unexpectedly tense and uncertain. "We can't do that."

"I know it's impossible, but you can try. We don't want to just give up and die."

"You don't understand. I don't mean—Jania, it's not a cave-in. It's not just you. It's everywhere. It's—we've been attacked. They've bombed us, Jania. All the tunnels are ruptured. Jania, we're buried alive."

"I—I—" Jania hunted for something to say and, when it became obvious no words would do, reached out and quietly severed the connection. Turning, she glared at Tedric. "I suppose you heard."

He couldn't help feeling at least a measure of the guilt she clearly expected him to bear. "I heard."

"Is it possible? Would you really do such a thing?"

"They might, yes."

"Then they did. I—" Suddenly, she laughed, but there was no pleasure in the sound. "They've buried you, too, don't you know? You must be expendable, Tedric. When they come down here and dig up our bones, you'll be just the same. Death is the great leveler."

Tedric shook his head, unable to respond. In the back, Nolan continued to curse in a soft, emotionless voice. Keller, so far, had not uttered a peep.

Jania clicked on the radio. She said, "My suggestions are as follows. Contact the imperial cruiser in orbit above. Ask to speak directly to the captain and—"

"The operations officer," Tedric said.

"The operations officer. Speak to him, find out their terms, haggle where you can, then accept them. Some will be saved. Maybe you. Not me. We thought they'd care enough not to kill us and we were wrong. Now cut our losses. Do as I say."

"All right, Jania," said the soft voice on the other end of the radio.

"And, Carla?"

"Yes."

"Don't let them know you're afraid. Be proud, if you can. Don't give them all the satisfaction."

"All right."

"Good-bye, Carla."

"Good-bye, Jania."

She cut the connection and leaned back in her seat and, for the first time, Tedric thought, she seemed on the verge of letting something show. He saw tears in her eyes.

Tedric faced ahead. A ton of rock. Two tons. Ten or maybe even twenty. There was no way out. He thought of the Scientists and their carefully conceived plans. How could they have known something like this? The answer was that they had not known, and their plans—along with his life—seemed doomed by circumstances.

Nolan tapped Tedric on the shoulder and, when he turned, said, "Then I guess this at least answers any questions we might still have had."

"Such as?" said Tedric, who was willing to accept any likely excuse to avoid thinking about those tons of rock so close ahead.

"Why Carey wanted to send us down here. We were diversions—I think that's obvious now. He sent us down here to be captured, to take their minds away from the cruiser up above, to lull them, and then he dropped his bombs. He murdered us. Too bad he won't pay. We will."

"Does it matter?" Tedric asked.

"Does it?" Nolan stroked his chin and laughed. "Hell, who knows? I enjoyed being alive. I guess I never thought I'd live forever."

"You seem willing to give up rather easily."

"And what else do you have in mind? Are you going to move those rocks all by yourself? Or will the Scientists help you? Them, and your sword."

"Let's not argue," Jania said. She seemed to have recovered from her tears. "Maybe we won't die. Maybe your friends will come and free us once they've got what they want."

"Tedric and I have no friends."

For the first time, Keller spoke. From his words, it was obvious he had been thinking for some time. "I believe there may be a way out," he said.

The other three, in unison, stared. "What can you know about that?" Jania said, derisively.

Keller flared, showing real anger. "I can know exactly as much as you know. Look, whether you like it or not, whether you're angry or bitter or full of hate because I refused to stay here and rot with the rest of you, whether you want to call me your husband or some blithering madman who likes to pretend he is, I don't care what you say or how you feel. But I lived here. I worked here. And I left. What did you want? Should I have stayed and ended up as you think, with no eyes or legs, buried deep in a tiny cavern, scraping away at the rocks with my bare fingers?"

"You could have refused to serve those who sent us here," she said stiffly.

"I serve no one but myself. I serve the Empire, and the Empire sent no one here. Have you forgotten? It was our parents. Our dear mothers and sweet fathers. They signed the papers. They collected the fees. It was them, no one else."

"Then you could have done what you promised. You could have saved your wages and bought my freedom, too. Do you know how many sisters and wives and daughters have rotted down here, waiting for some man to return and save them?"

"I wouldn't know, and I wouldn't want to guess. That's because it's a lie, Jania. I'm not paid. In everything but name, I'm still a slave. No one escapes from the imperial navy any more than they do from the mines of Evron. But at least in space I can breathe. I don't have a million tons of rock over my head. And that's something. That's a sort of a life."

"For you. Not for me."

"My wife," he said, as if it were a taunt.

"I . . ." She turned her head and for the first time looked squarely at him. There was a measure of defeat in her voice but also relief. "My husband."

Nolan cleared his throat. "I don't mean to interfere but, Keller, you did mention something about a way out and while I'm as eager as anyone to see your family tree resolved, I wish you might take a minute out and expand on that one point."

"Gladly, sir," Keller said, all business again, his anger and bitterness apparently forgotten. "What I was referring to is something Jania seems to have forgotten. They're called escape vaults and I know they reach all the way down to the bottom of the mines. If we could get to one of them and get inside, it could be a way of reaching the surface again."

"Well?" said Nolan, looking at Jania.

She was thinking. "Keller is right. I didn't think about the vaults. But they've been closed for ages."

"We played in them when we were children," Keller said.

"But the compression. And the pressure. If we tried to go up from this far down, we'd never survive the shock."

"What if we did it the way we did as kids? You know, slowly. In stages."

Again, she thought and, suddenly, brightly, a smile flashed across her face. "You know, it just might be worth trying."

Now, finally, with something resolved, Tedric decided to intervene. "Will one of you please tell me— me and Nolan—what it is exactly that you're talking about."

"Jania, you tell him," Keller said.

"No, you," said Jania. "You remember better than I."

So it was Keller who explained what the escape vaults were and how they offered an opportunity for four doomed creatures to think of life once again.

Keller said, "The vaults were dug originally in the first years of the mines, when the lodes were big and easily found. There are, I believe, four of them, east, west, north and south. Each vault is nothing more than a long vertical tunnel stretching all the way from the surface down to the deepest pits kilometers below. Each vault operates on air pressure. They were used originally to bring up ore without having to use the trains. When the first big lodes gave out and more tunnels were dug, the vaults were used much less. By the time Jania and I came here, when we were just children and hardly married a few months, the vaults were seldom used. In fact, we found out about them only by accident."

"We saw a sign," Jania said.

"That's right," Keller said, his eyes burning with a curious, excited light that seemed to show in Jania's as well. What could it be? Tedric wondered. Memory? The thought of the past? "We were riding a traincar to the northern sector when we both decided, without even talking, that we couldn't stand to work another minute and we hopped off the train when it slowed for a curve and ran away before anyone could see we were gone."

"They punished us."

"Locked us up and beat us half to death," Keller said, laughing, "but we really fooled them. We ran into a side tunnel and followed it, using our lights, and that's when we saw the sign."

"We could have gotten lost," Jania said. By now, the two of them spoke more to each other than to Tedric or Nolan. "It was very dangerous to wander in the side tunnels, especially then, when we were relatively new to the mines. I've known people to get lost and die and it's months before their bodies are found. We were young then. And confident. I don't think we were really afraid of anything."

"But we didn't get lost."

"No," she said, "because we saw the sign. There was an inscription printed in Galactic, but we couldn't read that. There was an arrow, too, which pointed—"

"Painted red," Keller put in.

"That's what we followed. The arrow led us into another side tunnel, where you could hardly stand straight up and down. We found the door. It was a heavy steel thing, but we were curious. At first, we couldn't budge the lock, but Keller found a sharp rock and we managed to pry it open."

"I don't think we even looked through." Keller laughed. "Hell, if we had, we would have gone running back, because it was just a drop, kilometers below. Jania went through first and I heard her scream. First a scream, then she was laughing, and I was already in after her. At first, I fell, too, but when she went flying past me, I knew it was all right. Then I was flying, too."

"You caught a handhold."

He nodded. "That was me. I wasn't crazy, not like Jania, so when I started shooting up through the air, I panicked a little and started waving my arms and that's how I ran into the handhold. They're long rubber pikes set perpendicular to the wall at every door. You wrap your body around one when you go past and that keeps you from sailing on to eternity. I grabbed the first one by accident, but after that we knew what to do."

"And I grabbed hold of Keller. That's what kept me from flying up, too."

Keller was laughing again, delighting in the recollection. "We went in," he said. "Fortunately, the air stopped rushing once we were out of its path, and, also fortunately, the door we'd landed near wasn't jammed like the first one, or otherwise we might be stuck in there still. We went through the door and found ourselves in another little tunnel. We walked along it and heard some noise and came upon a party of diggers. We were severely punished, but the foremen never did figure out how we'd managed to go so far in such a short time."

"And was that your only experience with these escape vaults?" Tedric said.

"Oh, no, sir," Keller said. "After that, we asked around and found out from some of the older ones what it must have been. We started to go back. Usually when we weren't working, which wasn't very often, but a lot of times when we wanted to hide, too. We found out that one side of the tunnel carried you up, but the other side, if you maneuvered over there, would bring you down. We found all four vaults and used three of them. The west one is the oldest and we never managed to get any of the doors open. But the other three functioned perfectly and we played in them for many months, maybe even years."

"Until you went away," Jania confirmed. "Until you left."

"And which one are we closest to now?" Tedric said.

Jania thought for a moment, then said, "Probably the east. We can't go west, as Keller explained, so it'll have to be east, I suppose."

Nolan couldn't keep quiet any longer. "East, west, north, south, who cares? Lead me wherever you want—just set me free."

Tedric wasn't quite that eager. There were a few

more points he wanted settled. "Can we be sure these vaults weren't also damaged or blocked by the bombing?"

"No, we can't," Keller admitted. "There's a good chance, because they were dug so deep and apparently made to last as long as the mine itself."

"And I don't believe you mentioned anything about the surface," Tedric said. "I assume you never rode all the way up."

"What would have been the use?" Jania said. "You can't escape a planet and if they'd caught us up there we would never have been allowed to use the vaults again."

"I understand that. My point is, we can't be sure the top isn't sealed off. The vaults are no longer used for hauling ore. Why bother to keep them open?"

"Why bother to close them?"

Tedric shrugged. "I see what you mean. The only way to know is to go up there and look. All right, then, let's do it."

"We'll have to walk," Keller said.

"I've never been down this deep," Jania said, "but I do think I know the right way to go. We may have to wander, though. It may take time."

"Time is something we can spare," Nolan said.

Jania glanced at the dashboard radio. "What about the others? Should I call and tell them what we plan?"

"No," Tedric said. "If we do manage to escape, it might be wisest if no one knows."

"And if we don't?" Nolan asked, bluntly.

"Then we're dead."

Keller, in the back, laughed and reached out to slap Nolan on the back. "But we're already dead, sir, so look on the bright side. We've got nothing to lose we haven't already lost."

The long walk through the dark, damp tunnels and caverns was no pleasure, but for Tedric at least it was a moment of extended quiet that allowed him time to collect and examine his own thoughts.

What surprised and concerned him most deeply was the effortless manner in which he had assumed authority over the party of four. Why him? When a decision had to be made, whether to abandon the traincar and seek out the escape vaults, the others had stood back and let him have the final word. He had no family. He spoke Galactic poorly. He was a barbarian, a man of action, not thought. Why not Nolan, with his famous ancestors, or even Jania? He and Nolan were, after all, still her prisoners. All he understood was that in a time of crisis, his mind seemed to operate with a peculiar clarity. He made decisions without knowing it—he took command without expecting it. In a way, this disturbed, perhaps even frightened him. Again, it was like some long buried thing reaching out of his past to take control of his present actions. But he was in the lead. He knew that and could no longer relinquish the reins. He knew it was his responsibility to do his best. If he failed, if they died, the blame could be shared with no one.

Suddenly, Jania, who walked slightly ahead of the others, stopped and swung her flashlight so that the beam struck the tunnel wall. "Here's one!" she cried. "It's a red arrow."

Tedric went over and took a look. The inscription in Galactic could no longer be read, but the arrow itself clearly pointed in the direction they were following.

"This is one of them?" he said. "You're sure?"

"The arrows down here mean nothing else. It's not like there's a lot of interesting sights to see."

"Then let's go," he said.

"There should be more."

She kept her light turned to the wall and soon enough uncovered another red arrow. There was a third. A fourth pointed down a narrow side tunnel.

"This way?" Tedric asked.

She nodded. "That's what it says."

The tunnel was so low that Tedric again had to duck his head to proceed. The steel door lay just around the first corner. They nearly went past it, unable to understand what they were seeing, when Jania stopped abruptly and cried out. "That's it! That's the vault! We've found it!"

Then she tried to open the door.

At first, it wouldn't budge. The heavy steel latch gave a groan and an ache but did not move. Keller tried but managed nothing more than she. Jania shined her light along the floor, searching for a loose rock.

"Let me try." Tedric came forward and caught

hold of the latch. He set his feet, tensed his knees, and jerked up. The latch gave with a loud groan, sprinkling rust through the air. Tedric pushed the door and watched as it swiveled open. Jania shined her light through, but there was nothing to see but darkness.

"I don't feel any rush of air," Tedric said.

"You won't. Till one of us jumps through. That's the only way to activate it."

"We won't go down? You said that each side of the vault forces the air in a different direction."

"The entrances are all on the up side."

Tedric nodded, leaned over, and peered through the opening. He stuck his head all the way inside the dark vault, but nothing happened. He reached below the door with a hand and hit an obstruction. It was one of the handholds Jania had described: a rubber pike as long as a man was wide. The others crowded in close behind Tedric.

He drew back and asked Jania, "When was the last time you played inside one of these?"

"Not lately."

"When? After Keller left?"

"No. Never after that."

"Then there's no sure way of knowing it'll even work."

"There's no sure way of knowing anything." She started to go past him. "If you want, I'll go first."

He held her back, not wanting to relinquish his leadership role. "No, I will." Turning, he put a leg through the door. Nothing happened, but he knew he would not turn back. He edged forward till he straddled the opening.

Jania put a hand on his shoulder. "Remember, don't try to do it all at once. It may be kilometers to the surface and your velocity will increase the farther you rise. Make use of the handholds. Stay close to the wall. If things get out of hand, if you start rising too fast and can't reach the wall, then try to maneuver your body to the other side. That'll make you start falling. You do it like a bird. Flap your arms and kick your feet."

"I'll remember." He looked at them. "Choose your own order to follow me. Don't anybody go until you're sure I'm all right. I'll yell or scream if everything's fine. If it's not, I won't utter a sound. I'll meet you on the surface."

"You're an optimist," said Nolan.

He started to reach back to shake their hands, but never made the move. That was too much like saying good-bye and the last thing he wanted was a brief farewell. He nodded, ducked his head, and came up on the other side. Then he swung his leg and, for a moment, sat in the doorway.

He used his heels to propel his body away from the wall.

He was falling.

For a long moment—too long—there was absolutely nothing. The air rushed past his head, screaming in his ears, but he knew he was just falling. It took all the effort of his will to keep from crying out. He tried to throw himself face down with his arms extended horizontally to present a bigger target for the up-rushing air.

Still, nothing.

Then it caught him. All at once. There was a rush of fierce air, then he was rising. It was as if the gentle hand of an unseen god had materialized to protect him. He rose slowly at first. He turned his head and watched until the open rectangle of the door appeared above. Then he screamed. He yelled. As he went past, he waved.

But, by then, he was moving too quickly and doubted that they had seen.

But they knew. They had heard him. And now they might be saved.

Tedric sailed. He didn't like gliding—during aircraft practice on the surface of artificial Nexus—but this was different. Here he needed no exterior restraints, no glider of wood, fiber, and canvas. He flew like a bird, like one of Carey's mythical blue eagles, and the pleasure he received was like nothing he had experienced before.

When the velocity with which he rose seemed to be getting excessive, when he felt himself losing a measure of control, he began to maneuver close to the wall. His eyes by now were sufficiently accustomed to the dark so that he glimpsed the rubber handholds as they flashed past. He tried to keep his body steady until one went past, then he kicked hard, sending himself rushing toward the wall. The next handhold caught him squarely in the midsection. He wrapped around it but held on tight. The wind whistled past and for a moment that disturbed him until he realized what a good sign that was.

The vault was working. There were others in the tunnel. Jania, Keller, Nolan. Soon they would all be free.

He briefly considered waiting for the others to fly past but decided that would only cause additional concerns he did not presently need.

So he let go. He floated. Then he rose.

After that, he followed a pattern. The higher he went, the greater his velocity seemed, so he stopped more frequently and paused for longer intervals. The air pressure affected his ears, and he knew if he lost his sense and rose too quickly it would kill him. The exhilaration of free flight made stopping difficult. It was like a scent of madness tempting him on. But he was patient. He knew how much he did not want to die. He hoped the others believed the same.

The whiteness, when it struck his eyes, was like a blinding flash of fire. He cried out in pain and only then realized what he was seeing. That circle overhead. It was—it had to be—the sun. They had spent the night underground, and now a brilliant morning stood poised outside to greet their return to life.

He sought a handhold, protecting his eyes with a hand, and when he reached it, hung on desperately while a wave of joy and relief washed over him.

He uncovered his eyes and, squinting, surveyed the wall of the tunnel above him. The handholds seemed to protrude more frequently here. He decided to go up one at a time till he reached the top.

He started out, rising with the air, stopping, rising again. The last handhold, thirty meters from the circle of light, led directly to a steel ladder. Tedric climbed slowly. When he reached the last rung, he rolled up and out and fell on his back and felt the cold, driving air of the surface rush past him.

He was alive. He was free. That was the difference.

He waited without moving till his energies seemed to return, then stood up. Ghostly cars and abandoned shacks surrounded him—equipment for receiving the ore from below—but there was no indication of life. He decided to wait for the others, then investigate. He kept his senses keen but nothing stirred. High above, a distant bird cried out. Insects chirped. These were friendly signs.

Keller came first. Unlike Tedric, he had neglected to take the last few meters slowly and came shooting out of the circle of the vault like a bullet from an antique gun. Tedric caught him and held him and Keller laughed and cried out, "We made it, sir! We made it! Ain't I smart? We found a way!"

Together, they waited for Nolan, who also came shooting out. Keller caught him and the two men cried and howled and slapped each other's backs.

Tedric waited alone for Jania. He leaned over the broad opening and peered at the darkness beneath, where nothing seemed to stir.

Keller eventually came over and said in a nervous voice, "That's just like her, sir. She'd be the one to take her cautious time, not come flying up like me or Lieutenant Nolan, risking our necks because we just can't wait."

But that explanation proved inadequate. Jania never did come. Keller insisted she had left just after him. "She was sitting in the doorway when I started going up and I waved. That was the last I saw of her."

He had passed Nolan on the way up, but neither had seen a sign of Jania during their separate ascents.

Keller wanted to go back down after her.

Tedric understood but said, "Either she's alive and will come up or she's dead and there's nothing we can do."

But Keller wouldn't listen to reason. He made a dart for the vault and Tedric had to restrain him.

Keller tensed, then relaxed, and he wept.

Tedric realized that Jania must be dead, and the thought gave him no pleasure. It was the first time (in this life) he had known·a friend to die. True, she had made them her captives. True, she was filled with bitterness and hatred. But he had liked and admired her and, what was most dreadful, her death made no kind of sense at all.

The effect was the same as when he had earlier killed the attacking stranger. It was like a physical blow, only stronger this time. He knew it wasn't just shock.

It was grief.

Tedric had never known that before.

7 WYKZL TREACHERY

To her immense surprise, Lady Rohann recognizes the old beggar dressed in dirty burlap and carrying a long parcel who has invaded the grounds of her palace garden. "Stay back," she tells the servants who have rushed to intercept the beggar. "I want to be alone with this man."

When they are together, seated beside a fountain where the songbirds cry above, Lady Rohann says, "Tedric, why have you come to my home dressed in disguise?"

"For your protection as well as my own. Seven times in the past three moons, supernatural beasts, creatures of black magic, minions of Sarpedium, have made assaults upon my life. In each instance, I have destroyed these beasts, but you lack the strength of my word and could be killed."

"Then why have you come to me at all? We parted and never expected to meet again." Lady Rohann is young, dark, slim, beautiful, as fragrant as a rose. Once, not long ago, she and Tedric were engaged to wed.

"Because, to my surprise, I am yet alive. And because, to my pleasure, I have found him again."

"Sarpedium, who left his castle."

"Ah, then you know of my quest."

"I have followed your progress." She shakes her head slowly, sadly. *"This means you must try to kill the wizard again."*

"It does, and so I have come to say good-bye."

Lady Rohann *rises to her feet, nostrils flaring with anger. "How dare you! Haven't I suffered enough before? Hasn't my anguish been great enough to suit you? I care nothing for your quest, Tedric. The world has long existed plagued by wizards and magic. Why must you risk every-thing to change what has endured so long?"*

"Because it is right. And because I have this." He held up the parcel in his hands. *"My sword, forged from the rock that fell from the sky."*

"But how do you know what you do is right? How do you know it will not bring more evil than good?"

"I know only what I must do," Tedric says softly.

Warrant Officer John Quill of His Majesty's Imperial Navy, decorated veteran of the Wykzl War, peered at the uncertain image that showed upon the lifeboat viewscreen and said, "I think that must be it there, lieutenant."

"On this damned thing, who could tell?" said Matthew Carey, turning away from the screen and making no effort to control his fury. In a blind rage, he slammed one fist hard against the plastic wall in front of him. "If this boat was equipped to carry a gun, I swear I'd use it to blast those monsters out of creation and to hell with anyone who said it was wrong."

"They are a deceitful bunch, sir," said Quill, who felt he knew the Wykzl well after ten years pitched combat in their vicinity. Quill was half-man, half-sub-man, but he had long ago adopted two names as an indication where his true loyalty lay. "You can trust them only to cheat and lie. They don't understand the meaning of truth. It's been a hundred years since I or any man set eyes on one, but they're not something a person forgets easily, I'll tell you that, sir."

Carey nodded half-heartedly and went back to his seat. Quill's opinion of the Wykzl held little interest for him right now. It was sheer frustration that was eating at him, and that was something he had seldom experienced in his life. He couldn't help remembering how well he had had things set up less than a full day ago. Then the Wykzl had intervened. He didn't want to hear about the Wykzl. Quill was starting to sound too much like one of Melor Carey's radio messages from Earth. There was an accusatory tone to his voice. *Don't underestimate the Wykzl. They didn't come all that way just to fly around and watch you operate. You were a fool to ignore them. I warned you before you left the Academy.* He had had enough of that for now. "Shut your mouth and do your work," he told Quill. "If I want any advice from you, I'll ask for it."

"Just giving you some background, sir," said Quill.

"Well, I don't want to hear it." The fact was,

though he hardly wanted to admit this himself, that he had blown it, and anything—Quill or anyone—was apt only to remind him of that sad truth. "What do you see on the screen now?"

"It's them, all right—the Wykzl lifeboat. They've got their pincers out now. I suspect we'll be locking in a minute or two."

"Then let me know when it's happened."

"Oh, you'll know it, sir. You'll feel it."

And what was he going to do then? That was the one point where his father's messages had remained vague. He had tried to ignore the Wykzl and failed in that. What was he supposed to do now? One way or another, he had to convince the Wykzl to get out of imperial space. The very presence of a Wykzl warship in this sector of space could be construed as an act of war. Was that what they intended? Could he pressure them with threats? The trouble was, he knew exactly why almost any man reacted the way he did. But a Wykzl was not a man. It was an alien monster, and how could he guess what made something like that tick? Quill, in spite of his constant babbling, was no help there. Carey didn't know how desperate the Wykzl were to obtain the Dalkanium they sought—he had already underestimated that desperation once—and he certainly had no idea why they wanted it.

From what his father told him, the situation had first arisen about two years ago. A message from the Wykzl had been received at the imperial palace in which they had asked for a large supply of Dalkanium ore. Melor Carey had managed to obtain that message and he had replied with a long list of conditions that must be met by the Wykzl before negotiations could even commence. Melor's response was in no way extraordinary for anyone with a trader's sense, but the Wykzl had never replied. That was two years ago, a nearly forgotten incident, when the rebellion had broken out on Evron Eleven and the Wykzl had suddenly appeared in the sky to observe.

Matthew Carey, sent here by his father to resolve the rebellion, had assumed that was all the Wykzl intended to do: observe. He had attempted to contact their ship on several occasions and received absolutely no response. In spite of this, obviously, his assumption had been mistaken: the Wykzl intended to do much more than observe. The real problem was he had no clear idea what to do next. It was the Wykzl commander, Mo-leete, who had requested this meeting in neutral space. Carey had had no choice but to accept the invitation. The mines of Evron Eleven were now buried beneath a thousand tons of dirt and rock dumped by the Wykzl bombs. He could only hope that some sort of enlightenment might emerge from this meeting.

There was a sudden thud.

The tiny lifeboat rocked from side to side, and Carey gripped the sides of his chair.

"That was them, sir," said Quill, from the viewscreen. "We're locked together."

"Then cycle the lock," Carey said bleakly, "and

let them on board. We may as well get this over with as soon as we can."

His original plan, he still firmly believed, remained utterly brilliant in its combination of deviousness and surface simplicity. For one thing, Phillip Nolan's presence aboard the *Eagleseye* had presented a definite problem from the beginning. Because of old family jealousies, Nolan could be counted on to cause trouble—he had confirmed that the day the trip began—but there had been no easy way of excluding him from the crew. It had been Carey's own idea to staff the *Eagleseye* with corpsmen from his own graduating class whose obedience and loyalty he need not doubt. But Nolan remained a problem, and so Carey had decided to use him—along with that strange man, Tedric—as a pawn in the first of his strategic moves. He sent Nolan down to spy on the rebellious miners and then made sure that he would be captured almost at once. He called the move a triple score. First, the capture of Nolan and Tedric gave him an easy excuse for taking any measures he wished against the rebels. Second, it neatly disposed of the problem of Nolan himself. And, third, it lulled the rebels into thinking they were safe from further attack. All of this had worked out perfectly, and he was convinced the rest of his plan would have succeeded as well. He had intended to launch a quick commando attack on the mines, capture and execute the rebel leaders, and, if they were still alive, rescue Nolan and Tedric.

But it hadn't worked out that way. Before he could move, the Wykzl had dropped their bombs. Now the mines were sealed up tight. And he didn't know what to do next.

His own thoughts occupied his mind so thoroughly that he failed to notice as the tiny side airlock slowly cycled open. When he turned to speak to Quill and found himself gazing up at a living, breathing representative of mankind's oldest enemy, he was too stunned to speak.

He had seen pictures, of course, but this was hardly the same. For one thing, the Wykzl stank. A peculiar odor, both musty and oily. Carey gulped and wished he could hold his nose.

The Wykzl stood half again as tall as a normal man. It was naked but covered from head to feet by a neat, pruned coat of pale blue fur. The face alone was hairless and showed a pink snout and two round red eyes. Above, where a man's eyebrows would have been, a pair of thin gray stalks, tendrils, fluttered in the air. The Wykzl hearing apparatus, Carey knew, was much stronger than the human ear.

"I am Mo-leete of the Wykzl," said the creature, in a perfect imitation of imperial Galactic. "I welcome you to the land of my species." The Wykzl stuck out his left paw and waited for Carey to shake.

Gingerly, as if touching something hot, Carey did so. The touch, peculiarly, was moist. "I'm afraid there's been an error," he said, as smoothly as possible. "This planet belongs to the Empire of Man."

"Ah, then perhaps that explains it," said Mo-leete.

"Explains what?" asked Carey.

"Your war-like intrusion into our sacred territory. May I suggest the likelihood of an error in astrogation."

"Our astrogator is a technician," Carey said coldly. "A robot. He cannot make errors."

"Then perhaps the fault lies with the chart-maker."

"I think not." Carey fought to control his anger. "My family has operated the mines on Evron Eleven since the conclusion of the war. For you to come here and claim otherwise verges upon a declaration of outright war."

"War with your family?"

"War with the Empire of Man."

Mo-leete made a deep clicking sound somewhere in his chest. He seemed to glare at Carey. "Are you threatening my ship?"

Carey feared that he had gone too far. "I was merely stating my position."

"Ah, yes, your position." Mo-leete clearly knew as well as Carey did that the *Eagleseye* was no match for the Wykzl cruiser.

Carey didn't intend to let the matter rest here. "Surely you won't deny that hundreds of human beings have died as a result of your attack on the mines. You were the one who took aggressive action, not me."

"But you were the one who refused to grant our original request for Dalkanium."

"That didn't give you the right to come here and take it."

"It gave us no right, but it did give us a certain need."

"Then what do you want the Dalkanium for?"

Mo-leete shook his head. "I am pleased to report," he said, ignoring Carey's question entirely, "that no one died as a result of our attack on the mines. The survey devices aboard our ship are far more sophisticated than yours, and it was an easy process for us to drop our bombs only in areas where no one would be harmed."

"And what do you intend to do now?"

Mo-leete nodded sharply, as if thanking Carey for finally coming to the point. "I am authorized to demand your immediate departure from this sector of space and further authorized to demand your written revocation of any claims you might have to the mines on Evron Eleven."

"That's impossible," said Carey.

"I'm afraid those are our terms."

Carey went over and sat down. Quill continued to operate the ship, apparently unaware of the discussion around him. Carey wanted time to sit and think. He didn't know what he had expected from Mo-leete, but it surely wasn't a frontal attack such as this. The Wykzl was leaving him no alternatives at all. His back was against the wall, and there was no place to turn.

"What if I promise to give you the Dalkanium you seek?"

Mo-leete shook his head. "You haven't the authority to do that."

"My father does."

"He's not here."

"I can contact him from the *Eagleseye*."

The Wykzl again shook his head, a strangely humanoid gesture. "Why should we accept a gift of what we have already taken?"

"And why should I allow you to take what is rightfully mine?"

"Because you have no choice."

"I think I have. You won't attack the *Eagleseye*. I intend to request additional naval forces. Unless you're serious about risking war, I don't think you have any choice but to leave."

"Then you are wrong."

"I don't—"

"Sir." It was Quill, speaking from the viewscreen.

Angry, Carey turned to tell him to be quiet, but something in the man's expression disturbed him. "What is it now?"

"I think you ought to come over here and look at this, sir. I think it may be important."

Carey looked at Mo-leete, but the Wykzl's expression was impossible to read. He went over to the viewscreen and looked past Quill's shoulder.

What he saw made him flare with sudden anger. There was another ship on the screen, a third ship, and it was considerably larger than either of the other two. Not a lifeboat, Carey knew, but a battletug. A Wykzl battletug.

He spun angrily around and glared at Mo-leete. "This is your ship here on the screen."

"It is."

"An armed battletug."

"Yes."

"Then you've violated the terms of our agreement."

"I could have warned you, sir," Quill put in. "They're not to be trusted. They're not."

Carey wasn't interested now in learning what people could have told him in the past. He came away from the screen and walked back to where Mo-leete stood. "What do you want from me?"

"Only the relinquishment of your claim to the mines."

"What good is something like that when it's obtained by threat of force?"

"What good is any agreement, Lieutenant Carey? Only as good as those who accept it. No, if I wished, I could easily seize the mines by direct force. Already, robots sent down from my ship are working to free the trapped miners. It would be easier for me if you do as I ask, but if you do not, nothing will change. This matter is too serious for us Wykzl to worry about being fair. I am authorized to run any risk, even open war, to acquire the Dalkanium we seek."

But why? Carey found himself thinking. This

time, he did not bother to voice the question; it was obvious Mo-leete would not answer. "Am I free to communicate with the *Eagleseye*?"

"You are free to do whatever you wish short of attempting to move your boat from this spot."

"And if I tried?"

"The battletug would open fire immediately and destroy you."

"And you," Carey said meaningfully.

"And me," Mo-leete admitted. "My crew will obey their orders. They have—"

Mo-leete broke off his speech in mid-sentence and fell into what seemed to be a deep trance. His eyes were glazed and his face went slack. Abruptly, his lips moved, emitting a strange sequence of gutteral clicks, clacks, and groans.

"That's their native language," Quill said, coming over.

"But who's he talking to?" It was plain by now that Mo-leete could no longer hear them.

"Probably his ship. Their tendrils can do that. They can pick up a sound over that much distance."

As quickly as the trance had come over him, Mo-leete regained full consciousness. He looked at Carey, then at Quill, and he blinked. "You have deceived us. You have lied."

"What are you talking about?" Despite the calmness of his voice, Mo-leete was obviously very angry.

"Your ship. Your cruiser. It has attacked my craft."

"But I didn't—it can't . . . Mo-leete, I promise you, I had nothing to do with it."

"Well, whoever did will pay. I have directed my crew to return your attack with full force. We will burn you out of the sky and see you die."

Carey could only stare at the Wykzl with open-mouthed astonishment. It was impossible. Captain Maillard would never dare exercise such authority on his own.

Quill had gone over to the viewscreen. Now he called to Carey, "Sir, I've got a picture now. He's telling the truth, all right. I can see both ships. And they're fighting, sir. They're fighting with everything each one of them has."

Carey groaned aloud and threw up his hands. He couldn't believe it—he couldn't believe anyone could be so stupid.

How was he going to explain this to his father?

He had not only managed to lose the family mines, but now it appeared he was about to lose the largest ship in the entire imperial fleet as well.

It was impossible. It was incredible. With Mo-leete, he went over to look at the viewscreen.

He saw it was true.

8 BATTLE IN SPACE

The old house on the bleak plain glitters with a foul, rancid light of its own, but the weary traveler on his mount does not appear to notice as he rides near.

He tethers his horse and slowly approaches the door. The traveler knocks once, softly. He appears to be a trader or merchant. He wears long golden robes and a well-trimmed blond beard. His hair is also yellow and cut short. He is a tall man, with broad strong shoulders, but he walks slowly, with a decided stoop. It is impossible to guess his age.

At his knock, the door opens. A beautiful young woman stands in the doorway. She is dressed in a thin, transparent white gown. Her teeth are long and sharp, and her eyes are yellow. She smiles with bright red lips.

"I—I thought this was an inn," the traveler stammers. "I didn't realize . . ."

Silently, the woman stands aside and beckons him to enter. Beyond her he can now see many other women. All are young, lovely, and nearly naked.

133

With apparent eagerness, the traveler hurries inside.

The door slams loudly shut behind him.

There is a staircase. It is long, wide, and winding. A peculiarly thick odor drifts down from above.

Without hesitation, ignoring the women, the traveler races for the stairs. As he does, his robe falls open, revealing the bulk of a longsword. The traveler clutches the sword and waves it in the air.

One woman jumps in front of him. There is fire in her eyes and death on her face. She raises her hands to block his path.

Tedric swings his sword from the hip. The blade whistles as it cuts the air. The woman's head flies off her shoulders.

There is no blood.

Tedric mounts the stairs.

Tedric surprised himself.

He had never really expected to come this far or, at times, to live this long, but now that it had happened and he stood where he did—in the central control room of the fleet cruiser *Eagleseye*—he understood for the first time why the Scientists might have chosen to send him here.

He liked the responsibility of command. He enjoyed the thrill of battle. He knew exactly what he should be doing and he went about it as if his life depended upon it.

He didn't understand why this should be true, but it was. In the past, some definite and specific rec-

ollection had always accompanied any moment of enlightenment. This time, as hard as he tried, he failed
to dredge one specific fact from his memory to con-
firm what he now firmly believed. But he knew. He
was certain. He had fought many battles in the past,
and he had won them.

There was no time to consider the matter more
fully. He had reached a tentative conclusion concerning his own reasons for being alive, but he knew he
must forget about that for now. Keeping careful
watch on the three narrow viewscreens located side-
by-side on the wall in front of him, he told Phillip
Nolan, who stood nearby, "We can't take this punishment much longer. Tell the astrogator to plot a
course using Evron's gravity as a whip. It's the only
way we'll snap their tractor beams."

Nolan nodded tightly and turned to one of the
two technicians occupying chairs in front of the opposite wall. Besides Tedric, Nolan, and the two robots,
the cramped control room contained three other figures. One was Assistant Steward Third-Class Keller,
another was Captain John Maillard of the Imperial
Navy, and the third was not a human being at all; he
was a Wykzl.

Tedric watched the leftward of the three viewscreens. It showed a scene of a metal surface gleam-
ing red with heat. Tedric knew that this picture represented the outer hull of the *Eagleseye*. The defensive
screens still protected the ship from the full force of
the Wykzl's powerful heatrays. Even so, Tedric well

knew, if they weren't out of here inside of a few seconds, the hull would melt and the battle would be lost.

The astrogator turned in his chair. "I have that course on lock, sir," the robot said.

"Then hit it," said Tedric.

"Now?"

"Now."

The screens jumped. There was no other indication of acceleration. The screens on the right and middle showed wavering patches of streaking stars. "Find the Wykzl ship," Tedric said. He kept his voice deliberately calm. "See if they're coming after us."

The second technician, the one who was not an astrogator, punched the keyboard in front of him. A moment later, in the center screen, Tedric saw the oblate globe of the enemy cruiser, its blue tractor beams and yellow heatrays flashing impotently through the void. As he watched, the outline of the ship grew fainter. "We've got a headstart," he said.

"They didn't know we'd run," Nolan said.

"They knew," said Tedric. "They didn't know just when."

But the image of the other ship was already growing again. Tedric knew this meant he was being pursued. He also knew this was exactly what he wanted. "More power," he said softly. "I don't care if the engines burn."

Nolan shook his head. "There's no way we can stay ahead of them for long."

"It doesn't have to be for long." Tedric pointed to the left screen, which still showed the crimson hull of the *Eagleseye*. "Just long enough for us to cool off."

Nolan went over to consult with the technicians, relaying Tedric's instructions.

Tedric, standing alone, gazed at the viewscreens: the burning hull, the pursuing ship, the maze of the stars. He was aware of what he was doing: risking the lives of an entire ship's crew because of something he only vaguely remembered being told. Did he really have that right? What if he was mistaken? What if the Scientists were wrong?

So far, they hadn't been. The Scientists had not failed him. He could only hope this would not turn out to be the first time.

Nolan came back. "They've still got the velocity."

Tedric nodded coldly. "As long as we stay ahead."

Escaping from Evron Eleven had proved difficult enough in itself.

The first problem was recovering from the shock of Jania's death.

Needless to say, it was Keller who was by far the most deeply affected.

While Tedric and Nolan sat on the ground, conversing occasionally in hushed tones, Keller wandered off to be alone. He sat down some distance away from the others, his back turned toward them, his posture tense. Tedric made no attempt to interfere. He knew whatever Keller was feeling and thinking now, it had to remain a private matter.

Finally, after an hour had passed, Nolan said, "I

really don't think we can afford to wait much longer."

Tedric looked across to where Keller still sat. "No, I suppose not."

"We have no clear idea of what's going on. Someone might stumble upon us. We can't afford to be captured again."

"No."

"Maybe you could talk to him. I'd do it myself, but I have no idea what I should say."

Tedric had no better idea. Still, Nolan was right. Something had to be done. "All right. I'll try."

Standing, Tedric went hesitantly over to where Keller sat. "May I have a word with you?" he asked softly.

Keller turned at the sound of Tedric's voice. His face was like a hollow mask. His eyes showed the depth of his private pain. "Sir?"

Tedric crouched down. It seemed easier to talk this way. "Nolan thinks it's time we were moving out. I can't really disagree with him."

"Might be dangerous here, huh?"

"I think it's a possibility."

"Could you . . . ?" Keller faltered before going on. "Could you give me another minute, sir?"

"Do you think it will help?"

"I don't know, sir. I don't know if anything will."

"If she's dead, Keller, nothing can bring her back."

"Oh, I realize that. You see, that's not really what hurts—what hurts the most. The whole time I've been over here, I've been trying to reason this thing out. Not that she's dead. Not how she died. It's me I'm worried about. You saw how she acted when she first saw me. It was like she didn't even want to know that I still existed. That hurt me, sir. That hurt me more than anything in my life."

"But once you explained your reasons, she said she understood."

"Did you believe her?"

The blunt question caught Tedric by surprise. He tried to answer as truthfully as he could. "I don't think she would have lied."

"Maybe not. But maybe, too, it's not her that's most important. Maybe it's me. I know what I did was wrong. I knew it when I left her and I know it just as plainly now. It was wrong of me ever to leave her in this place. It was selfish."

"I never said what you did was right. Nor did I say it was wrong. That's not the kind of question I can answer easily. I just said I believed I understood."

"Maybe so, sir, maybe so, but the fact is that it seems so damned senseless. There was no more reason for her dying here today than there is for me being alive. What can I do about it?"

"Go on, I suppose."

"As if nothing had happened? As if I'd never set eyes on her for the last time? I can't do that, sir. I can't be the same old happy and laughing Keller again. That guy is dead now. Maybe he never was really alive. Maybe all he ever was was a lie."

"Sometimes there's a good reason for telling a lie."

"For living one?"

Tedric nodded. "Even for that."

"Then you think I should go on?"

"I think you should try."

"Because she would have wanted that?"

"I can't speak for her. Nor for you. But I think it's what you want."

"Maybe so."

Tedric stood. "I'll give you another minute."

"Thank you, sir. I appreciate that."

Tedric went back and sat down beside Nolan. "Well, what did you say to him?" Nolan asked.

"I don't think it was what I said. It was what he said. I just listened."

"Then he's coming?"

"In another minute."

When Keller rejoined them, he seemed almost exactly the same as always before. He laughed and he joked and he made no mention of Jania or her death. But Tedric knew he hadn't forgotten. Keller was a strong and determined man. The shell he had built around himself to conceal his real feelings was thick and smooth. But there were glimpses. In his eyes. Keller's eyes never wholly hid the truth.

They went away from the hole through which they had escaped the mines but hadn't gone far when they came across a group of robots who seemed to be busily engaged digging a new shaft deep into the planetary surface. The noise of machinery alerted

them before they actually reached the site. Keller led
Tedric and Nolan toward the concealing shadows of a
large rock. "Those robots don't come from the *Eagleseye*," he said.

"Then where do they come from?" Nolan asked.

Tedric had an idea. "I think we've been neglect-
ing something."

"What?"

"The *Eagleseye* isn't the only ship in orbit around
this world."

"The Wykzl," said Nolan.

Tedric nodded. "Yes, exactly."

"Are you sure?"

"No, but can you explain these robots any other
way?"

"Then we may have been wrong. In blaming
Carey, I mean."

"I'm beginning to think that's possible." Tedric
leaned forward, watching the robots digging their
shaft, working a pulley machine and emptying buck-
ets of rock. He was beginning to realize the depth of
the error he had made by disregarding the Wykzl
presence here. The more he thought and the longer
he watched the robots, the more certain he became
that it was the Wykzl, not Carey, who had bombed the
mines. But why? What motivated them? Why were
they even here? He didn't know the answers to these
questions, but he did realize how critical they might
be. If he could understand the Wykzl, he would know
much more than a few specific facts.

Nolan, clearly, was thinking along similar lines.

"But if they did bomb the mines—if the Wykzl did, I mean—then why are they trying to free the survivors now?"

"Maybe they don't want them dead."

"Then what do they want?"

"The mines."

"But surely there's a sufficient supply of Dalkanium within the Wykzl sphere."

"Do we know that?"

"They never ran out in five hundred years of warfare."

Tedric shrugged. "There's only one way of finding out. We'll have to ask."

"A robot can't tell us."

"Then we'll have to wait for the robots' masters to arrive."

They had waited. Till nightfall, and then beyond. The robots continued to work. Daylight meant nothing to them. Finally, a brilliant light ignited the sky. Tedric, Nolan, and Keller huddled close to their rock as a Wykzl shuttlecraft fluttered to the ground. A crew of four emerged and disappeared at once down the newly excavated mineshaft. The shuttle remained perched on a flat rock, surrounded by a circle of harsh yellow light. A few robots wandered listlessly, deprived for the moment of their meaningful labor.

Nolan looked at Tedric. "Should we go now, or wait?"

"Better wait. We're not armed. I'd rather take on

a Wykzl than a robot. At least they're made of flesh."

"The robots won't harm us, sir." Keller had remained subdued. It was clear he was thinking of Jania, whom he had found at such a cost and then lost again.

"How do you know?" Tedric asked.

"It's in their programming. Once, I guess, during the war, they tried to use them as soldiers. It seemed like a good idea and they killed a lot of imperial soldiers, but it nearly backfired. They swarmed down on some of the Wykzl's own worlds, killing and killing. They were ones we had captured and reprogrammed. It wasn't nice and the Wykzl learned their lesson. They never used robots again."

"How do you know all this?"

"I've run into these robots before. This isn't the first time the Wykzl have gone sneaking around the Empire. They just don't talk about it. Nobody wants another war. Not them, either, I think."

Tedric nodded thoughtfully. What Keller had reported was interesting, but it was something to be pursued later. "Then you think we ought to go out now."

"The robots won't even notice us. They're programmed to dig holes, nothing more."

Tedric decided to accept Keller's words. He stood up and went forward alone, but the few robots remaining in the vicinity behaved exactly as Keller had predicted. When that became obvious, he stopped and motioned the others forward. The lock hung open in the bottomside of the shuttle craft and they crawled through.

Inside, they found a wide-eyed Wykzl staring at them.

It took all three to overcome the alien. Tedric was amazed by the strength of the thing. He didn't want to kill it, but there seemed no other way of keeping it from fighting back. He finally managed, while Nolan and Keller held the Wykzl's hands, to get around behind and fasten a hold on the creature's throat. It seemed to have a need for oxygen. After another long struggle, the Wykzl gagged, kicked, thrashed, then fell still.

"Is it dead, sir?" asked Keller. He squatted on his knees and wiped at the stream of blood running from his nose.

"I hope not." Tedric stumbled through the shambles of the cockpit, searching for something with which to restrain the Wykzl before it recovered consciousness. He finally decided to use his belt and those of Nolan and Keller.

Nolan was awake but unable to speak. He lay on his back and heaved great sighs of breath. Tedric got the belt off his own waist and, with Keller's fumbling assistance, managed to tie the captured Wykzl to a jutting protrusion on one wall.

Then Tedric went over to the cockpit control panel. It had not been damaged during the fight but, from his first glance, it might as well have been. The problem with the control panel should have been obvious: it was an alien control panel.

Tedric didn't have the slightest idea how to fly this shuttle.

Keller reached past his shoulder and fingered a red plastic lever. "You start with that, sir."

Tedric turned, open-mouthed. "You know how to fly this thing."

"Not perfectly, no."

"Well, how well?"

"Well enough to get it into orbit."

"But . . . how? This is a Wykzl ship. Surely you've never been given lessons."

"Well, I . . . actually . . ." Keller climbed into the high chair that fronted the panel. His legs dangled a full meter off the floor. "It's supposed to be a secret, sir, but there was an expedition—two years ago—we went into the Wykzl territory."

"Why?"

"That part I never knew myself. Maybe the officers did—though I think not. We visited a half-dozen of their planets and took pictures. We were prepared to fight but they never interfered. They knew we were there—probably knew why, even if we didn't—but they let us alone."

"That is odd," said Tedric.

"But not new." Nolan had picked himself off the floor. His face showed bruises, and his upper lip was cut. Otherwise, he seemed capable of staying alive. "I've heard rumors of that expedition—my family has. The Emperor probably didn't know about it. The Careys ran the whole thing."

"Matthew Carey?"

"His father, more likely. Matthew may have known, but I doubt it."

"But you don't know what it was all about?"

"No idea at all. Reconnaissance in the event of future war was the supposed explanation. I never bought it. We're too weak to fight anybody and the Wykzl aren't especially interested, either. Why should they? They beat us once."

Tedric decided to file this information for future reference. There were more immediate matters to attend to now. Like getting away. If the other four Wykzl happened to return before they were gone, they wouldn't stand a chance.

"Keller," he said, "get us out of here as fast as you can."

Keller continued to study the panel in front of him. "That's just what I'm trying to do, sir." He reached out and rather tentatively stroked the lever he had earlier shown Tedric. There was a moment of anticipation and then, above their heads, the reassuring hum of an engine. "So far, so good, sir. Our instructions in operating these things weren't too complete. They just wanted a few of us to know in case we had to steal one, like this. But I have a good memory."

"Then put it to use and let's get out of here," Nolan said impatiently.

Keller reached for another lever. "I recommend you hang on, sirs. This may get a bit bumpy."

The flight upward from Evron Eleven proved as precarious and exciting as Keller had predicted, but somehow—Tedric never quite remembered exactly how—the Wykzl shuttlecraft not only managed to vacate the surface of the planet but actually achieved a successful orbit around it. Finding the *Eagleseye* was no simple problem, in spite of its mass, but Nolan managed to calculate a tentative position and Keller, struggling with the alien instrument panel, reached that position. The great fleet cruiser, like an inflated bag, filled the entirety of their one miniature viewscreen. Tedric, balanced securely in a perch between the control panel and a wall, motioned Keller away from his chair. "I think we can safely drift now," he said. "The *Eagleseye* will notice us eventually, and they can draw us in."

Keller nodded and sprang from his seat. The satisfaction he felt showed on his face, and Tedric thought it was well deserved. Keller pointed at the captive Wykzl, who remained securely bound in a corner. "Maybe I ought to tell him it's finally over." He grinned. The Wykzl had not uttered a sound during the entire ascent, nor had he once dared open his eyes. "I think I may have frightened him out of a couple hundred years of life."

"Don't tell me you can speak the Wykzl language, too," said Tedric, who by now was growing accustomed to Keller's countless wonders.

"No, sir, but they can speak Galactic. Nearly all of them. My instructor explained it was because each one lives so much longer than we do—a thousand years to a Wykzl is like a hundred to us. They have more than enough time to learn anything they want."

This revelation made Tedric feel slightly uncomfortable. He couldn't think of anything he'd said that the Wykzl should not have heard, but nonetheless the idea of an alien eavesdropper disturbed him. "Do you think you can get him to talk to us?"

"You mean torture?"

"Well, nothing that drastic."

Keller shook his head. "Then there's no way. The Wykzl are tougher than the hardest steel. The planet where they originated is like the worst jungle you can think of, except that it covers the world and can't be tamed. That's how they beat us in the war. They're so mean and stubborn, they refused to admit we were beating the hell out of them till, suddenly, everything changed and they won."

"Did your instructor tell you that, too?"

"No, sir," said Keller, with his best ingenuous grin. "That one I figured out for myself."

Tedric was still interested in trying to converse with the Wykzl, but before he had a chance to try, a green light in one corner of the control panel caught his attention. The light was flashing brightly. "Now what?" he asked Keller.

"That's the viewscreen." Keller wandered over to the panel and began striking buttons with what seemed to be utterly random hands. "Somebody's trying to call us. Must be the *Eagleseye.*"

When Keller finally managed to achieve a clear picture on the tiny screen, it showed the face and

shoulders of a young navy lieutenant. This surprised
Tedric, who had rather expected Captain Maillard or
even Matthew Carey himself. Then the lieutenant, in
a nervous voice, said, "You have exactly four minutes
in which to surrender or be destroyed."

"The idiots!" cried Nolan.

"Well, answer them," Tedric told Keller. "Make it
clear who we are."

"Carey's behind this," said Nolan.

Tedric shook his head. "Even he can't know who
we are."

Keller's fingers flashed up and down the control
panel, and Tedric finally realized that, while Keller
had indeed uncovered a picture and voice, he still
didn't know how to return the transmission. Nolan,
also aware of the situation, came over and stood stiffly
behind Keller. "Damn it, do something! Is this the
way you want to die?"

"I'm trying, sir. I really am." A desperate, frantic
look took control of Keller's eyes. His hands never
ceased moving. "I'm trying everything I can think of."

"I thought you said your memory was so damned
good."

"Good, sure, but not perfect."

Tedric couldn't help smiling, but the lieutenant
on the screen, who had remained silent for some
time, now interrupted to say, "You have exactly three
minutes in which to surrender or be destroyed."

Nolan threw up his hands. "I surrender, damn it!
I do!"

But that wasn't good enough. Keller's crazed fin-

gers continued their dancing act, with no apparent
success. Tedric's glance roamed from the screen to
Keller and back again. Nolan paced in agitation, while
even the Wykzl had opened its eyes and appeared to
be aware of what was going on.

The lieutenant spoke to warn that they now had
only one minute in which to surrender or be
destroyed.

But finally—with some thirty-nine seconds remaining to their lives—Keller shouted, "I've got it!
We can transmit."

Nolan rushed over to the panel and began insist-
ing that he was human. Keller shouted, too, waving
his very human hands high in the air.

Even then, after all the show, the lieutenant was
not wholly convinced. Tedric calmly suggested that
he consult with someone aboard who knew them better. The lieutenant resisted this advice at first, plainly
suspecting some bit of alien trickery, but finally went
away and came back with Jonay Shortley, a corpsman
from their graduating class. Tedric and Nolan spoke
in turn, and Shortley, after a painful moment's hesitation, confirmed that the voices and faces on the
screen did indeed resemble those belonging to Nolan
and Tedric.

The lieutenant reluctantly consented to let the
Eagleseye pick them up.

Tedric told Keller to break the connection only if
he was sure he could do so without losing it for good.
Keller confidently asserted that was no problem.

When they reached the *Eagleseye* and cycled through the airlock, they were met by a party of sub-men sailors armed with heatguns. The head of this party was none other than the same nervous young lieutenant they had previously met via viewscreen. There was a moment's consternation when the sailors caught sight of the high, bobbing head of the captive Wykzl, but a shout from Nolan prevented them from opening fire at once. Tedric then asked to be taken to see Matthew Carey.

The lieutenant shook his head stiffly. "I'm afraid that's quite out of the question."

"You mean you still think we're Wykzl in disguise," Nolan put in.

"I mean, simply, that Lieutenant Carey is no longer aboard the *Eagleseye*."

"Then where is he?"

"He is presently aboard a lifeboat in open space meeting with the commander of the Wykzl ship."

"Whatever for?"

"To arrange surrender terms, I suppose."

"Ours?"

The lieutenant frowned. "Theirs, I suppose. They bombed the mines on Evron Eleven. I suppose you wouldn't know about that."

"Know about it? We were there when it happened," Nolan said.

"Perhaps we ought to report to Captain Maillard," Tedric said.

"I believe he is interested in talking with you."

"Then take us to him." Turning, Tedric motioned to Keller, who stood off to one side, a hand on the arm of the Wykzl prisoner. "Bring him along, Keller."

The lieutenant hung back for a moment. "Are you sure that's safe?"

"I think we've got him outnumbered," Nolan said.

"These things can be awfully sly sometimes."

Nolan winked. "So can we."

That testimonial seemed to convince the lieutenant, who motioned his men to fall into step. He then led the way up through the inner corridors of the great ship toward the control room that lay at its core.

Tedric tried to decide what and how much ought to be told to Captain Maillard, but he had trouble concentrating on the problems of the moment. He was getting another of those strange feelings again, the sensation that something vitally important was about to occur without any firm knowledge of what that vital thing might be. He knew it must have something to do with the meeting now being held in space between Carey and the Wykzl commander. But what?

The central control room of the *Eagleseye* was far less impressive than Tedric had anticipated. It was a high-ceilinged, circular room, barely large enough to hold the three men who already occupied it. As Tedric and Nolan squeezed into the room, one of the men came forward to greet them. It was Captain Maillard. Tedric and Nolan halted and saluted their superior officer.

"Glad to have you men back," Captain Maillard said. He seemed almost embarrassed by their presence. "Carey told me you had been—" He stopped and his eyes grew large. "Where did you get that thing?"

Tedric turned around. Keller and the Wykzl prisoner had just entered the room.

Tedric turned back, smiling. "We managed to capture him during our escape from Evron Eleven."

"That must have been rather difficult," Maillard said dryly.

"It was a rough fight, for sure. Take a look." Nolan stuck out a lip. "You can see for yourself where I nearly lost a set of teeth."

The intrusion of Keller and the Wykzl forced Maillard back toward his seat. He dropped down in front of the three high viewscreens and gazed up at Nolan with an expression equally composed of wonder and worry. "But wasn't that a rather risky move to make? I'm not sure that Carey would approve. He's in their hands this moment. We can't have him harmed as an act of revenge."

"I don't think there's much chance of that, sir. Once peace has been made with the Wykzl, we'll naturally have to let this one go."

While Nolan talked about peace, which Tedric failed to see as a very likely occurrence—the Wykzl still held the upper hand here—Tedric switched most of his attention to the three viewscreens. The first two showed surface views of the planet below, probably the site of the mines, although the actual picture in both instances lacked enough detail to be sure. The middle viewscreen, in contrast, showed a section of starlit space. There were two small ships in the center of the screen and a third, somewhat larger one just entering the picture from the right. Tedric studied this screen with rare intensity until at last he understood exactly what it must mean. He was about to alert the others to the danger he had perceived when he stopped, suddenly staggered. This was it, he realized, with a start, and his hands grew cold.

What he was seeing on the screen, he was seeing for the second time in his life. Oh, not exactly, no. Even the Scientists were not omnipotent. But they had told him of this moment. Forewarned him. And, more than that, they had told him exactly what he must do in consequence.

He let Nolan continue talking, describing for the benefit of Captain Maillard the thrilling details of their adventure on Evron Eleven. Tedric circled behind. He first checked the door, and saw that the lieutenant along with at least two of his guards still lurked there. The other two men in the room appeared to be only technicians. They operated complex keyboards that seemed to control the ship's central nervous system. Tedric continued to circle. Only when he stood directly beside Captain Maillard, with his hand close to the other man's sharp sword, did he speak.

Tedric cleared his throat and couched his revelation in the softest possible terms. "Sir, have you looked at the viewscreen lately?"

Maillard turned, and Tedric turned with him. It was Nolan, though, who first understood the meaning of the screen. "That's them," he said. "The two lifeboats."

Maillard nodded, still not understanding.

"But they're not alone," Nolan said. "There's a third ship there. It—"

Tedric decided to finish the sentence for Nolan. "It's a Wykzl warship."

He waited for Maillard's instant reaction and then moved. Maillard shouted and made a move as if to rush the screen. In a swift, sleek, graceful motion, Tedric reached out and drew Maillard's sword cleanly from its sheath. He put an arm around Maillard's chest to restrain him and laid the swordblade against his neck.

"If anyone moves," Tedric said, "I will cut his throat."

Maillard gasped. Nolan took a step forward, then stopped, his mouth wide open in astonishment. Keller appeared shocked and stunned, while the Wykzl, his eyes open, seemed only curious.

In the corridor, the lieutenant and his guards had their heatguns drawn.

"I mean you, too, lieutenant," Tedric said. "I especially mean you."

"Don't—don't come closer," Maillard choked.

Tedric had known from the moment he moved that he could never succeed alone. He had been forced to act first, because only he was fully aware of what must be done. But he would need Nolan's help. And Keller's.

Tedric looked at Keller and said, "Go close the door and lock it. We don't need anyone in here but ourselves."

Keller hesitated. He looked at the door, at the sailors and their guns, then back at Tedric. "Sir, this could be called mutiny."

"I know what I'm doing, Keller. I give you my word this is for the best."

Keller looked to Nolan for help. "Sir?" he asked.

But Nolan was looking at Tedric. "Can you tell me what you're doing?"

"I want to save that ship."

"Matthew Carey?"

"And the Empire."

"How?"

"By launching an attack against the Wykzl cruiser."

While everyone else showed their surprise, including—with a rather dangerous gasp—Captain Maillard, Nolan nodded, as if this was what he had anticipated hearing. "Tedric, are you sure you know what you're doing?"

"I was told to do it."

"They'll blow the *Eagleseye* out of space."

"I know how to beat them."

"How? Were you told that, too?"

Tedric couldn't be sure. The idea was in his mind but where he'd gotten it he couldn't be sure. "I was told."

"By—" Nolan hesitated, clearly unwilling to say the word. "The Scientists told you."

Tedric nodded.

Nolan still wasn't sure. Clearly what he had to decide was whether Tedric, his friend, was a raving maniac or truly possessed of some special knowledge. Nolan stepped toward Keller, paused, then slipped suddenly past him. He stood at the control room door and pointed at the floor.

"Lieutenant, I want you and your men to drop your weapons. Guns and swords. Lay them at my feet."

The lieutenant's hand went toward his waist but stopped there. Tedric carefully drew the blade of his sword closer against Maillard's throat. Maillard obediently gave a little cry.

"I don't know whether Tedric is madder than a red moon or saner than both of us put together," Nolan said, "but I do know that he isn't bluffing. The punishment for mutiny and murder is the same. There's nothing to make him stop now."

"Lieutenant, do it," Maillard said, as if responding to a cue. "Drop your weapons. I don't want to die."

With an official command on his side, the lieutenant no longer had a reason to hesitate. He drew his sword and let it fall to the floor. His heatgun and those of his men followed with a rhythmic clatter.

Nolan bent down and picked up one of the heatguns. He kicked the remaining weapons inside the control room. Then he stepped past the door and made a motion with his gun. "Lieutenant, let's go."

"Phillip, where are you going?" Tedric called after him.

"To find a nice, quiet place to store these fellows. If we're going to pull off what you've got in mind, we won't want any blabbermouths alerting the crew."

"That's a good idea, Phillip." But Tedric felt hesitant. He did not want to be alone. But he could trust Nolan. Couldn't he?

Pointing his gun, Nolan led the lieutenant and his sailors away. Tedric felt suddenly vulnerable, impatient for his friend to return. Keller helped his mood improve by picking up one of the discarded heatguns, bouncing the weapon neatly in his hand, and grinning. "This is going to be enough fun to make discorporation worth it." Tedric hoped he was half right—about the fun.

Nolan came back alone. He closed the control room door, then locked it securely. "All right, Tedric," he said, folding his arms and leaning against the door, "I think you ought to give us a few facts."

Tedric nodded and lowered his sword. Free at last, Captain Maillard dropped to his knees, gasping and choking. Tedric felt miserable. He hadn't intended to humiliate this rather harmless man but

there had been no other way. Tedric stepped around
Maillard and picked up another of the guns. He
glanced at the middle viewscreen and saw that the
Wykzl battletug now loomed dangerously close to the
two oblivious lifeboats.

"There isn't much time for talk," he said.

"I understand that," Nolan said, "but I do think
you owe Keller and me whatever you happen to
know."

Tedric nodded and pointed at the center screen.
"Well, that much you can see. The Wykzl have not
kept their word. They intend to capture our lifeboat
and hold Carey and the other man hostage in return
for our promise to leave the area."

"Carey was a fool for trusting them."

"If that's what he did," said Tedric, who could
never regard Carey as a fool. "But whatever anyone's
individual motivations, there's obviously only one way
of blocking the Wykzl's ploy. We have to attack first
and beat them."

"And you think you can do that?"

"Yes, I do."

"But there's still one factor I don't quite understand. What makes this so important? Even if we do
lose Evron Eleven, what of it? You and I don't suffer
and neither, to tell the truth, does the Empire. It's the
Careys who will be hurt and I don't think either one
of us worries much about them."

Tedric was shaking his head. "I wish I could tell
you everything, Phillip, but there are things I hon-

estly do not know myself. All I can tell you are my feelings and even they are not entirely clear. But I don't think Evron Eleven really enters into it. I don't think the Scientists are concerned with who owns the mines. But I do know, as surely as I've known anything in my life, that they want me—us—to fight and defeat the Wykzl here. Your interpretation of why that is important is as good as mine. A chance for the Empire to regain a measure of self-respect? A chance, simply, for you and me to do the same? I don't know, Phillip. I just don't."

"And I don't care," said Keller, who seemed unconcerned by this talk of the mysterious Scientists and their ambiguous concerns. He came over and laid a hand on Tedric's shoulder. "All I know is that this man helped save my life and I owe him at least that much in return. If he gets discorporated, I just hope I'm sitting in the next chamber when it happens."

Nolan threw up his hands. "All right," he said. "If it's good enough for Keller, then who am I to argue? I'm with you, Tedric, and I'll say just one thing more: I sure as hell hope, for your sake as well as mine, that you're right."

"I am, Phillip."

"Then let's go."

Tedric was ready. The first thing he did was go back to where Captain Maillard knelt and help him to his feet. He said, with sincerity, "I'm sorry, sir, that it was necessary to treat you so badly. I know you can't place your trust in me the way my friends have, but I want you to know that what I'm doing is for the good of the Empire, if nothing else."

"Only the Emperor can say what is good for the Empire," said Maillard, with surprising decisiveness. "You are only a man, the same as I."

"I am a man who seeks to be of service to the Empire."

Maillard, less than convinced, shook his head sadly. "You have chosen a poor manner in which to conduct your search."

"I'm afraid I'll have to be the judge of that."

"No. Not you. Only the Emperor may judge."

Tedric turned away, seeing the uselessness of further argument. He approached the two technicians who, through all the turmoil swirling around them, had sat steady and alert at their controls. "Men," Tedric said, "in a few moments, I intend to order the *Eagleseye* forward into battle with the Wykzl. I can't guess how you feel about what I'm doing, but I do know this: if you fail to respond to any of my commands, then none of us will live to see another day. Can I count on your immediate obedience?"

Both robots turned and looked at Captain Maillard, who had gone back to his chair. Maillard returned their glances with a sharp nod. "Do as the man says. I doubt that he's right, but I can't prove that he's wrong. Obey him as you would me."

Grateful but aware that Maillard would not appreciate a formal thank you, Tedric took up a position in front of the three viewscreens. Nolan came over and stood at his side, while Keller remained close to the door with his Wykzl captive. Tedric ordered the technicians to provide him with a clear straight-ahead view from the bow of the ship on the left screen and a view from the stern on the right. He kept the center screen fixed as it was on the lifeboats and approaching battletug. "Which of you is the astrogator?" he asked.

"I am," said the closer of the technicians.

"Then I need an immediate favor from you. Inspect your local charts and find a star known as 2X49."

"I am familiar with that star," the astrogator said stiffly, as though his professional reputation rested on the matter. "Its present location is approximately six parsecs from here."

"Then place an alternate lock on that star. When I give you the signal, that's where we're heading as fast as the ship can go."

"That star is a black hole, sir. If we head for it, we'll be sucked inside."

Tedric nodded. "I know what it is." He spoke as stiffly as the astrogator had earlier. "What I want is a lock that'll bring us as close to the hole as we can go without being drawn hopelessly inside. Can you manage that?"

"I can, but it's never safe. The mass of a black hole is constantly increasing. If I miscalculate the rate of that increase, we'll be gone."

Tedric shrugged. "Do it. It's worth the risk."

Nolan showed a glimmering of hopeful interest. "Then you do have a plan, Tedric."

"I said I did, didn't I?"

"It involves this black hole?"

"It may." He wasn't trying to be deliberately vague. There just wasn't time to discuss his intentions now. Turning to the other technician, the one who wasn't the astrogator, he gave the order to accelerate the *Eagleseye*. Within a matter of moments, he could see in the motion of the stars in the left and right screens that the giant ship was moving forward. He placed a second order, alerting the crew for imminent battle. The fight of a lifetime—of many men's lifetimes—was about to commence.

Now, as the *Eagleseye* continued its reckless dash through space, with the pursuing Wykzl cruiser still falling farther and farther behind, Tedric turned back to his astrogator. "That star I told you to keep on alternate fix. What's its present location?"

"Point seventeen parsecs."

"Then edge us toward it. You're going to have to do it surreptitiously. I don't want them to know what I'm doing."

"Edge?" said Nolan. "We can't edge anywhere at this velocity."

"That's why we're stopping."

"But they'll catch us."

"I want them to."

"Are you crazy?"

Tedric shook his head. "No, I don't think so."

Nolan stared at him. There was a long moment of deep silence, then finally Nolan laughed, breaking the tension in an instant. "I don't think so, either."

"Then you're with me?"

Nolan waved at the control room. "Who am I to dissent?"

Tedric understood his meaning, and felt pleased. The mood of the control room had subtly altered the moment the *Eagleseye* first exchanged tractor beams with the deadly Wykzl craft. The technicians—even the astrogator—called Tedric *sir* now, as though his assumption of command had been something other than mutiny. Captain Maillard, although he had not openly participated in the battle, had been heard time and again shouting words of encouragement. Tedric knew this was by no means extraordinary; battle often did that to men: it drew them together—transformed separate individuals into a unified team. Even fighting on opposing sides could do that—Tedric felt a strange appreciation of the captive Wykzl all of a sudden—and fighting on the same side could push that closeness into something approaching oneness. Tedric realized in his own case that this was true not only for the few men in this control room but for the hundreds of sailors and corpsmen spread throughout the huge ship. He wondered if they felt the same and ached to stand beside them, where the real thrill of battle must lie, not here in the command post, far removed from the omnipresent threat of sudden extinction. He knew that most of the men on board this ship, as well trained as they doubtlessly were, had come to serve with little expectation of ever putting their military training into practice. For them, this had to be a real chance, and most must comprehend, consciously or not, that such a chance might never come again. Tedric thought that might help explain it: how the *Eagleseye* had withstood the pressure of the initial Wykzl counterattack so well. He felt proud of his men. As severely battered as it was, the *Eagleseye* still soared on.

The ship had already begun to slow. With Nolan, Tedric watched the center viewscreen as the Wykzl cruiser gradually grew in size and bulk. A tentative tractor beam shot out from its bow, probed briefly at the void, then disappeared. It wouldn't be long, he knew. First the tractor beams, then the heatrays. "Lift the shields," he commanded, and without looking back heard his order relayed by a technician to the rest of the ship. The Wykzl ship was as big as his clenched fist now. A tractor beam flicked out, probed. Suddenly, in the screen at the center, he saw a flash of blue.

The technician said, "Sir, we've been caught."

"Keep slowing," said Tedric.

"Are you ready to maneuver?" asked the astrogator.

"Wait till they're closer. Wait till they're throwing their heatrays and concentrating there. Then use everything we've got to get us aside. I mean everything."

"Yes, sir."

The ritual of deep space combat had in no way altered since the last battle between men and Wykzl a century past. In fact, in the last thousand years, there had been little change in the manner two ships battled to surrender or death. The cruisers met in the void. Tractor beams, which acted like the clinging webs of killer bugs, drew the ships together in a deadly embrace. Then the heatrays. Blastguns. Neutron bolts. Vibradarts. For protection, each ship erected a defensive network of quarkian shields. If these collapsed, as ultimately they must for any cruiser, then actual boarding might follow—hand-to-hand combat as vicious and merciless as any known since the dawn of formal warfare. Tedric had already decided he would not permit this last to occur. If the shields fell and left the *Eagleseye* vulnerable before he completed the maneuver upon which hinged any hope of personal victory, he knew he would surrender immediately. He could bear the pain of failure and defeat, but the deaths of too many innocents were much harder to carry.

Tedric watched as a brilliant yellow bolt of fire burst from the side of the Wykzl cruiser. Seeing this and knowing it represented only the opening volley in a concentrated heatray assault, Tedric commanded, "Return their fire." He knew full well the relatively impotent weapons of the *Eagleseye* had no chance of penetrating the sophisticated Wykzl shields. Still, it was necessary, for his own men as well as the enemy, to keep up the pretense of trying. "Hit them with everything we've got."

"Bow and stern, as before, sir?" asked the technician who controlled the guns.

"No," Tedric said. In the initial engagement, he had directed his beams without effect at the most vulnerable points of the Wykzl's shields. "Run a sweep. Hit everywhere."

"We'll never break through that way," Nolan said.

Tedric shook his head. "I'm more concerned with keeping them busy."

The viewscreens showed a stunning display of brilliant color. There were white stars, blue tractor beams, yellow heatrays, black space, scarlet shields.

"The hull is heating up already," Nolan said, pointing to the center screen. "The shields must have been damaged during the first attack."

Tedric asked the technicians, "Can either of you men give me a reading on how long we can last without burning up?"

"I'll get it," said the technician. Tedric made an effort to recall their names. The astrogator was Essell. The other was Deekay. This was Deekay. The names of creatures with identical features were difficult to remember. Deekay punched some buttons on the panel in front of him. "Sixteen point fourteen common minutes. Barring further deterioration in the shields."

Tedric knew there was little chance of that: the shields, now that they had been penetrated, would surely continue to weaken progressively. The sixteen minutes, practically, could not be much more than another ten. He turned to the astrogator, Essell. "What about 2X49? When will we reach our locking point?"

"Fifteen point twenty-seven at our present rate. I activated the lock as soon as the first tractor beam caught us."

"We'll have to increase power and hope they don't catch on to the maneuver."

'I have increased power. We're at maximum thrust now."

"And that's as fast as we can go?"

"The Wykzl tractor beams are stronger than they ought to be. They've had a hundred years to work on them. We can't expect all our facts to be up-to-date."

Tedric frowned and looked back at the center screen. He studied the rippling red hot surface of the hull and thought it might be best to surrender now. The technicians couldn't be wrong. Figures did not lie. His brilliant plan—the Scientists' plan—had fallen short because of a single miscalculation: the Wykzl were stronger than anyone had known.

A hand touched his shoulder. Tedric turned and found himself staring eye-to-eye with, of all people, Captain Maillard. "I couldn't help overhearing your conversation with the technician."

"Well, it is your ship, sir."

"That's not what's important now. I just had a thought. Am I correct in deducing that it is your desire to lure the Wykzl into a certain sector of space and that because of the deterioration of the shields you will be unable to do so?"

Tedric nodded. "Basically, that's the way it is. You see, I thought we'd be able to do it quicker, pull them through space on their own tractor beams. I was wrong. I should never have tried it. I'm not only a mutineer, I'm a failure at it." He didn't know why he felt the need to justify himself to this man, but maybe that wasn't the point. He was justifying himself to himself and that was still important to him.

But Maillard seemed less concerned with Tedric's mistakes and more interested in his facts. "But the difference is only a few minutes, correct?"

"A few minutes or a few centuries. If the shields fall and the hull is burned, it doesn't matter what time the calendar says."

"I think it does matter."

"Just what are you getting at?"

"Simply this. I'm an officer in the Imperial Navy. I've made a study of past battles, participated in a few of my own, and learned something of the tactics of space warfare. And there is a certain maneuver. It was used during the war for just the purpose you envision: to draw another ship through space by its tractor beams without severing the connection."

"Well, what is it?"

"A spin. Turn the ship over and over, bow to stern. The motion weakens the tractors and allows an increase in mutual velocity. If you can spin the *Eagleseye* as I've described, you ought to reach your locking point before the shields fall."

Tedric looked at the technicians. "Well, is it possible?"

Deekay was already punching his control panel. He looked up at Tedric. "It may be."

"Then let's do it. Let's spin."

"What about the gunners? Should we continue to fire our heatrays?"

"Yes. It'll have to be a diversion. I still can't afford for the Wykzl to guess what we're doing. We have to keep them busy."

"Firing during a spin can be dangerous," Maillard said. "You may end up slicing your own ship in half."

"We'll have to risk it."

"I can't delay another minute," Deekay said. "I have to know your decision now."

Tedric consulted only with Nolan. When Nolan finally nodded his assent, Tedric said, "Give the orders. We're going to try a spin."

There was no doubt in anyone's mind when the maneuver began. Even here in the core of the great ship, Tedric felt the change. Normally, the *Eagleseye* rotated along its horizontal axis at a velocity designed to create a feeling of Earth standard gravity aboard ship. Now, spinning vertically as well as horizontally, the ship lost this artificial restraint. Objects floated through the air. Captain Maillard lost his balance and sprawled on the floor. In two of the viewscreens, the blanket of surrounding stars whirled madly past. Tedric gripped the wall in front of him and held firm. It had to work—it must.

"Are we maintaining our lock?" he asked the astrogator.

"It's firm, sir," said Essell.

"And our rate."

"It's increasing."

"Can you give me an estimate?"

"Six point fifteen."

"Till locking point?"

"Yes, sir."

Tedric refused to feel any measure of triumph. There was a possibility now, a chance of winning out, but it was far from settled. Would they figure out now what was happening? He had counted on the heat of battle to distract the Wykzl, but the spinning maneuver had surely confused them. Tedric realized all it took was a ship's astrogator bright enough to take a look at the character of the surrounding stars. Once they realized the true nature of 2X49, that it was a black hole, they would never come near it. Still, he experienced a deep renewal of faith. The Scientists once again had not failed him. Of course, they could not possibly have known in advance that Maillard would step forward to save everything. Or could they? Tedric tried to remind himself that the Scientists were not magicians or prophets. They were men, wise men, but merely human. They were not infallible. Only very close to it.

Tedric never took his eyes away from the viewscreens during the entirety of the *Eagleseye*'s tumbling flight through the void. Everyone else in the control room, excepting of course the technicians, remained similarly transfixed. Because of the spin, the screens at best could only show the Wykzl cruiser for brief, flashing moments. But it was still coming, still attacking, still firing. Essell, from his panel, confirmed that the vessel had in no way altered its natural course. Tedric crossed his first two fingers. The gesture was an odd, silly thing he had picked up from someone at the Academy. He glanced at Nolan and saw that his fingers, too, were crossed.

Then it happened. The *Eagleseye* righted itself and the spinning stopped. Floating objects dropped to the floor with a loud clatter. Tedric felt a sudden lessening of tension in his stomach.

"Locking point, sir," said Essell.

"And the Wykzl ship?"

"I'm trying to locate it now. It seems . . ."

"Are we still being hit?"

"Yes, sir."

"What about the shields?"

"Less than two minutes," put in Deekay, who seemed to have that figure close to the top of his mind.

"Wait—there it is!" cried Nolan.

Tedric looked up at the screens and finally found what he wanted on the left. It was the Wykzl ship, but something was wrong. Even as Tedric watched, the ship seemed to be getting smaller, drawing gradually away.

"It's pulling away," Nolan said.

"No." This was Essell, from his controls. "It's being pulled away."

"Pulled?"

Essell nodded. "By 2X49."

"This soon?" asked Tedric.

"If we were a thousand kilometers closer, we would be, too."

Tedric watched the viewscreen with a feeling that approached awe. Somewhere in that picture, he knew, lay the invisible star, 2X49, a black hole, an object so massive and so shrunken that even light could no longer escape its surface. And the Wykzl ship was being drawn downward, down into that. The Wykzl captive, also understanding, let loose a choked sob, as if from pain, the first sound Tedric had heard him utter. And that pain, Tedric knew, was caused by him. It was his maneuver that had thrown the Wykzl ship inside the gravitational field of 2X49.

But he couldn't say he was sorry. There had been no other way. If there had, wouldn't the Scientists have told him?

"Attack has ceased," Deekay reported.

Tedric could see that on the screen. Still visible and within easy firing range, the Wykzl had withdrawn their weapons. He had to admire that. It was quite possible the Wykzl could have doomed the *Eagleseye* along with themselves. They had not done that. "Tractor beams?"

"Only weakly. I think the Wykzl are clinging. We're the only thing keeping them free."

"They can't possibly draw us in with them?"

"Not now, no."

"But they could have, at one time?"

"At the very beginning, when they were close to us, yes, it was possible."

"But they didn't."

"By the time they realized what was occurring, they were too far away."

Tedric wasn't sure that was true. Who could ever hope to read the alien mind of a Wykzl? Not a robot technician, that much was sure. What if they had known, in time? They had still not chosen to act. The Scientists must have known, too. They had said nothing to Tedric about this final danger. Maybe the Scientists knew how the Wykzl thought. Maybe they knew that these creatures, even when they were vicious, could never be cruel.

"We'd better get out of here," Tedric said softly. He told his technicians: "Fix a lock on Evron Eleven. Align the screens for a sub-space run. There's nothing else here for us to see."

But there was one other thing—whether Tedric wanted to see it or not. Even as he spoke, in the corner of one eye, he saw the left viewscreen. The Wykzl ship, like a weak flame, suddenly went *poof*. One moment it was there—a gleam of light against the background of stars—and the next it was not. The Wykzl ship had been swallowed up. Consumed by a cosmic mouth. And the crew? Were they dead? Living? Transformed into some entirely new state of being? No one knew the answer to that. There was only one way of finding out—by entering the black hole. And no one had ever done that and returned to speak of it.

"Hit it," Tedric murmured. "Get us out of here."

The others had seen, too. "That was awful," Nolan said.

"Yes, but it had to be done. They would have fried us to death without a second thought."

"I suppose so, but that's war—that's expected. What we did to them—it was different somehow. Worse."

"I know what you mean," Tedric said, even though he wished that he did not. Turning, he faced the figures behind him. The Wykzl had recovered from its momentary anguish and the others seemed simply stunned, as if awaiting further direction. Tedric knew he had nothing more to provide them. "We've won," he told them as calmly as he could. "We've beaten the enemy—destroyed them."

The others responded with nods, if even that. There was no joy in the room, no exultation in victory. Tedric understood the impact his words must bear: for the first time in a century, ships belonging to the Empire of Man and the Wykzl had met in battle; the imperial ship had won.

Now Tedric came forward. He approached Captain Maillard and raised a hand to his forehead, saluting. "Sir," he said, "I am your prisoner."

Nolan came forward, too, though he seemed less eager than Tedric. He reached for his holster, removed the heatgun, and with a sigh, handed it to Maillard. "Me, too," he said softly.

Across the room, Keller's gun clattered to the floor. "I'm with the lieutenants," he said.

At first Maillard made no move. He seemed taken by surprise. Tedric knew he had underestimated this man. Maillard was certainly no fool. "I accept your weapons, gentlemen, and I return them." With a sweep, he held out Nolan's heatgun, forcing him to take it back. "I also assign you to immediate duty. Lieutenant Tedric, Lieutenant Nolan, Steward Keller, until further notice to the contrary, you will serve here in the control room as my special assistants."

"Thank you, sir," Tedric said, as surprised as he was pleased.

"What for?" Maillard said. "After what you've done, no matter how you've done it, I can't very well lock you in the brig."

"Not you, maybe," Nolan said. "But Matthew Carey can. And he will. You don't know him the way I do. Once he has the excuse, it'll be the discorporation room for us for sure."

"Not if he doesn't find out. Not if he knows nothing."

"But how can you keep that from him? What happened out here was pretty obvious."

"To us, perhaps. To him, not necessarily. I'm willing to take all the responsibility for the attack. The responsibility and, I'm sorry to say, the glory. Carey may be angry for a time, but I am especially adept at playing the part of the fool. Carey may guess the truth but he will be able to prove nothing."

"What about those other fellows out there?"

Keller put in. "The guards. They saw us. What's to prevent them from telling Carey?"

"And what's to prevent me from saying it was all a vast misunderstanding. I'll ask that you men be disciplined. Two weeks apiece confined to quarters. No man has yet been discorporated for a mere misunderstanding."

Nolan was shaking his head. "Captain Maillard, I fear I've made a mistake about you."

"Most men do." Maillard winked. "But that's what I want them to do." Turning, Maillard went over and stood behind his technicians. "When we've reached our locking point at Evron Eleven, I want you to locate the lifeboat with Matthew Carey aboard. Let me know when you have a lock on that."

"Yes, sir," said Essell and Deekay, as if they were one.

Maillard put an arm around Tedric's shoulders and steered him toward the viewscreens. "Maybe we ought to rehearse the story we're going to tell. Any ideas?"

"No, not really."

"Well, good. Because I have some. I have plenty." And Maillard laughed.

9 MO-LEETE'S STORY

When Tedric reaches the end of the wide, winding staircase, the space in front of him dissolves into a bottomless pit inhabited by formless shapes that lunge at his eyes and tear at his flesh.

Ignoring these unreal things, he trudges forward. Lifting his sword high above his head, he speaks boldly: "Sarpedium, black wizard, I am Tedric, Lord of the Marshes, the ironmaster of Lomarr. Do you think your magic will conceal you from me forever? Come out from wherever you hide and prepare to meet your end."

There is a wall of orange fire that washes over him like a great wave.

Tedric laughs. "Your magic cannot harm me, sorcerer. I dare you to come forward. Stand for your life."

There is a scaly dragon as big as a mountain that lumbers forward on clawed feet.

Tedric smiles.

There are women more beautiful than any he has

179

known who dance, whirling naked, tempting him to follow.

Tedric grins.

There is a serpent coiled in a circle, endlessly swallowing its own tail.

There are devils.

Demons that shriek.

Vampires that howl.

To all these things, Tedric shakes his head. He laughs.

Then he strides toward them.

Methodically, waving his sword, Tedric chases each spirit away.

Until, finally, he is alone with one other thing. It bears the shifting shape of a human being.

"You are Sarpedium," says Tedric.

"I am he," says the shape, without pride.

"I am Tedric."

"Yes."

"You fear me."

"No." But the shape trembles—it is a lie.

"You fear me because I will kill you, and I will kill you because you are evil."

"I, Tedric, or you," says Sarpedium.

"Perhaps neither of us, wizard. The true evil may lie only in what has spawned you: fear, superstition, uncertainty. When you are dead, when magic is at last banished from this world, then men may live as free men once again and lift their eyes boldly to the sun."

The shape—Sarpedium—lets out an awful howl and tries to rush past Tedric. The ironmaster is too quick. His sword rises, and it descends.

After much discussion aboard the *Eagleseye* and the exchange of several heated messages with the imperial court on Earth, a select party was finally formed to go down to the surface of Evron Eleven and accept the official surrender of Mo-leete, the surviving commander of the Wykzl cruiser.

Mo-leete himself, who had been permitted to go below to supervise the robot rescue operation, was the primary reason behind all the bitter discussion. The Wykzl had been quite specific concerning the makeup of any surrender party. He wished to meet with Tedric, Phillip Nolan, Keller, and Captain Maillard.

He did not wish to meet with Matthew Carey.

"The Wykzl are a very ritualistic species," said Captain Maillard, in an attempt at mollifying Carey. "I have no more idea than you why Mo-leete wants to meet with whom he does. We were aboard the *Eagleseye*. You weren't. Perhaps, in terms of his beliefs, that's all that's really significant."

"But he's the one who's surrendering," Carey said. "It's not us. What makes him think he can get away with dictating the terms?"

"Apparently, the Emperor agrees he should be granted that right," Maillard said. "We did receive a message to that effect transcribed in his private code."

"The Emperor wasn't aboard the *Eagleseye*, either," said Carey, who clearly put little store in what the Emperor did or did not want.

"I think the important thing is to make sure that Mo-leete and the rest of his people get out of the

Empire of Man as quickly as possible."

"I think the important thing is to make sure we don't let them think they can push us around."

Tedric, who was present at nearly all these heated discussions, thought he knew what the whole thing might well be about. It was that other Wykzl, the silent captive who had observed the entirety of the space battle. He had known, as Carey did not, the true events that had occurred that day, and by now, since he, too, had been sent down to Evron Eleven, Mo-leete must also know. Maybe the Wykzl commander was simply curious to get a close look at the men who had vanquished his ship. Maybe there was something more to it than that. Tedric didn't know. He did know why his name was included and Carey's was not.

Tedric, Nolan, Keller, and Maillard used a floater capsule to reach the surface of Evron Eleven. Tall piles of dirt and rock rose to greet them, ghostly mountains in the stillness of early morning. The Wykzl robots had nearly completed their excavation of the mines. Many hundreds of miners had been saved and only a few dead bodies had been found. The rescued miners had been sent immediately by shuttle to the orbiting *Eagleseye,* where most of the ship's medical facilities had been set aside to tend to their care. The eventual fate of the miners was still undetermined. They would be returned to Evron Eleven and expected to work once the mines were repaired, but that might take months and even years.

Tedric wondered if even the Careys could force the miners to return to that hell underground once they had become accustomed to the light of day.

Mo-leete emerged from a metal shack and crossed the landscape to greet the shuttle. Tedric recognized the Wykzl commander from his trappings. He was not alone. The Wykzl with him, though Tedric could not be sure, seemed to be the same one Tedric had captured at this spot what now seemed like years ago.

"What do we do?" Nolan whispered in Tedric's ear.

"We go out and say hello," Tedric said.

"This place gives me the creeps."

"Maybe it's supposed to," said Captain Maillard.

By the time the four of them stepped out of the shuttle, Mo-leete and his companion stood waiting at the foot of the ladder. There was no sign of recognition in either of the aliens. They stared into blank space, as if they lived alone on the planet.

For a long moment, all of them—men and Wykzl —stood uncomfortably face to face.

Tedric at last decided to interrupt the silence. "Mo-leete, by authority of His Majesty, Kane IV, we have come to accept your surrender."

The Wykzl cocked his head, as if straining to hear sounds from faraway. Finally, bowing his head, he acknowledged the presence of the others. "I surrender my honor to your hands." He spoke in perfect Galactic and, as he did, dropped suddenly to his knees. Even then, his head was barely lower than Tedric's throat. Slowly, as if the motion were one requiring a great expenditure of energy, Mo-leete reached toward the heatgun at his waist.

Beside Tedric, Keller let out a gasp of surprise and reached for his own holster. Tedric gripped his arm. "No," he said. "It's all right."

The gesture Mo-leete was about to make was one familiar to any human being.

He gripped his heatgun by the butt and held it out to Tedric. "This is yours, sirs. My right to bear it is vanquished."

The other Wykzl had so far not budged an inch. Tedric looked at him, rather than at Mo-leete, hoping somehow to discover what move he ought to make next. Before coming here, he had tapped the ship's central data bank for any information it possessed regarding Wykzl surrender ceremonies. There was absolutely nothing to be found. If any Wykzl had ever surrendered to any human being, that piece of information had never been transmitted to another.

Tedric knew he would have to act from intuition alone. Bending down, he took the huge alien beneath the shoulders and casually lifted him back to his feet. "Your honor is yours, Mo-leete. I have no proper right to demand it."

It seemed to be the right move to make. Mo-leete again bowed his head but in agreement this time, not submission. "You are a merciful conqueror, Tedric."

"Thank you."

Mo-leete caught Tedric's hand in his and squeezed tightly. He shut his eyes and spoke in his native language. Then, in a softer tone, he translated. "Let it be known to all that, from this day onward, the human being known as Tedric shall be recognized as a lord among all Wykzl and that, from the petty being known as Mo-leete, he shall receive all the favors, service, and honors properly possessed by that rank." Mo-leete opened his eyes and spoke to all of them. "In other words, my friends, whenever you need me, you need only call."

Tedric was willing to accept Mo-leete at his word, though he couldn't help wondering: how far did that promise go if the two space nations met again in war? He decided not to pursue the subject. "You have my respect, too, Mo-leete."

"And mine as well," said Captain Maillard, step-ping forward and inserting his hand between those already clasped. Again, it seemed to be the right ges-ture at the right time. Nolan and Keller clasped theirs, as well, and for a moment, his own hand held by four others, Tedric felt a stirring of some deep emotion.

Mo-leete was the one who broke his grip first. Stepping back, he lifted his head and Tedric sensed that the purely ceremonial aspects of the surrender were now at an end. Mo-leete returned his heatgun to his waist and, as he did, his entire body seemed to shed the tenseness it had possessed, as though a long ordeal had finally been ended. "You fought a remarkable fight in space," he said. "My brother has told me of it."

Tedric shook his head. "We tricked your crew. That was all. If you had been aboard ship, the outcome might well have been different."

"Ah, yes, certainly." Mo-leete seemed to possess few doubts on this point. "But I wish no human being death or harm. Please sit." He pointed to the ground. "I will explain."

Tedric searched until he found a relatively flat spot, then dropped to his haunches. The constant beat and wail of nearby machines hidden from view by the mounds of disgorged dirt pounded in his ears. For any of them, it was necessary to speak in an abnormally loud tone to be heard and understood. A lone robot suddenly darted through their midst. It swept past and climbed one of the mounds as easily as if it wore wings.

"I believe," Mo-leete said, "that I may have angered several of your superiors by requesting this meeting with you."

"It angered Matt Carey, if that's what you mean," Nolan said.

"Ah, yes, that youngster." It was odd how easily Mo-leete's apparently inhuman visage managed to communicate such human emotions: now he radiated a certain amused contempt. "But surrender is an important rite among my people, perhaps because it is performed so infrequently. The defeated is permitted only to share his honor with the true victor. Matthew Carey was not aboard your conquering ship. For him to have joined your party would have violated the sanctity of the rite and made true surrender on my part impossible."

"Tell that to Matthew Carey. He thinks whatever he wants to be true has got to be true."

Mo-leete nodded sadly. "A very intense individual." It was clear that, for him, this could never be a compliment.

"But you promised to explain things to us," Tedric said. "We don't even know what brought you here in the first place. It wasn't conquest, was it?" He spoke these words so quickly, even before he had a chance to realize consciously that he intended to speak, that his own voice caught him by surprise. For a moment, he suspected another of the Scientist's hidden implants, but at last decided to blame his own curiosity. It wasn't the Scientists who needed the answer to the question he had asked—more than likely, they already knew—it was himself, Tedric.

"We came for the obvious reason," Mo-leete said. "In an attempt to capture this planet's supply of Dalkanium."

He spoke in a matter-of-fact tone that made it difficult for Tedric not to believe him. "But surely the available supply within your own nation is sufficient to meet your needs."

"Normally, yes," Mo-leete said, almost wistfully. "But these are not normal times."

"I don't understand."

"No, of course not, and that is why I am willing to explain. Still, there are certain concepts difficult to translate from my language into yours. One such concept is the 'honor' that we now share together. In my language, the word means far more than that. Another such concept is the . . ." He paused, still seeking the correct word. "The invaders, the clouds. Have you heard previously of any such thing?"

Tedric shook his head, as did the others, even Keller. "I don't know what you're talking about, no."

"Then I will begin at the beginning," Mo-leete said, "which would be some eighteen of your common years before now. It was at that time that the first of the invading clouds was discovered inside the boundaries of my Wykzl nation. At the time the cloud was no more than a few hundred thousand kilometers in diameter and regarded as purely an astronomical phenomenon. It wasn't until some months later that our observers realized that the cloud was expanding."

"By cloud," Captain Maillard said, "do you mean just that?"

"No," Mo-leete said quickly. "No, it is not a cloud. It is—" He held up his hands. "You must see one to understand. Its color is a bright, almost fiery red. From a distance, it appears to be quite solid, but when seen from close-up, a certain transparency is visible to the naked eye."

"Then it's just a dust cloud," Nolan said. "That's nothing extraordinary."

"So we, too, thought at first," Mo-leete said, and again there was a wistful, nearly nostalgic note to the way he spoke of the near past. "As I said, the cloud grew. And not slowly, either, not gradually. Within less than a year it had swollen to the point where it occupied a portion of space more than two parsecs in diameter. It had also swallowed up two star systems. One of these was occupied—by Wykzl."

"The inhabitants were not harmed," Maillard said.

"We do not know."

"But you must know," Nolan said. "Why didn't you contact them?"

"Because the cloud—the invader—would not allow it. As for the Wykzl swallowed up inside the cloud, none has ever been heard from again. Our most sophisticated instruments are unable to penetrate the clouds. It is as if—inside—there exists nothing at all."

"You said clouds," Tedric said. "The first one wasn't the only one?"

"No. Within the Wykzl nation, more than two dozen have now appeared. Some, like the first one, now occupy as much as fifty light-years of space. Others can still be measured in the millions of kilometers."

The more Mo-leete spoke, the more strongly Tedric experienced a rather peculiar sensation: it was like a cold chill running up and down his spine. This story of invading clouds was not something remote and removed from him. He knew it was important. Important to him alone.

Mo-leete went on, "And, because of these clouds,

we Wykzl have experienced an unexpected and dire need for Dalkanium. Two clouds have recently materialized within the star cluster that includes the bulk of our population. At their present rate of expansion, these two clouds, along with the others already discovered, will within a century succeed in swallowing up more than ninety percent of all living Wykzl. In other words, sirs, my race is threatened with something very close to ultimate extinction."

"And how will the Dalkanium help you?" Maillard asked.

"By allowing us to increase the size of our space fleet. Evacuation is our only weapon, massive evacuation, the removal of billions of bodies through hundreds of parsecs of space. Will the clouds merely pursue us wherever we go? For myself, I think the answer is yes. But we have no choice. We cannot simply wait and die."

"But these clouds can't pursue you," Maillard said. "You talk almost as if they were conscious entities."

"We believe that they are."

Only Nolan laughed aloud, but the sound died quickly on his lips. It was obvious that Mo-leete was more than serious. To him, the extinction of his own species could never be a joking matter.

"Do you have any evidence to support this rather extreme claim?" asked Maillard.

"We have the evidence of our own senses. The clouds have spoken to us."

"In words? With their mouths?"

"In—again, I have trouble expressing a concept. In thoughts . . . images . . . photographs. Horrible things. When a cloud approaches a planet to be captured, the inhabitants there begin to see the most monstrous things. They go mad, in mass, long before they are swallowed up."

Maillard seemed less than eager to pursue this subject, and Tedric could understand why. It seemed a bit too fantastic even for a universe in which all things were deemed possible. Mo-leete was clearly afraid of the clouds, with probable good reason. Fear alone could cause some strange delusions. "But why have these clouds appeared nowhere else in the Galaxy?" Maillard said.

"We have reason to believe that they have. In the Bioman sphere. Contact with the Wykzl and the Biomen was, as you know, long ago severed. But reports have reached us, transmissions."

"But there has been nothing in the Empire. If there had, I think I would have heard of it."

"No, that is true. Nor have the clouds appeared among the Dynarx heathen. To us, that is only a sinister sign. Why have the clouds appeared only within the boundaries of the two most advanced species in the Galaxy?"

Tedric couldn't help smiling at Mo-leete's condescending attitude. Had the Wykzl forgotten so soon the purpose of this meeting here? But he had a question to ask, as well, one that was—again, he knew this for certain—vitally important in a very personal way. "Are we the first men to learn of these clouds?"

Mo-leete shook his big head with obvious sorrow. "Alas, you are not, which is the reason for our terrible battle here, I am sure. At the time we became fully aware of our crucial need for Dalkanium, we naturally attempted to acquire an additional supply through peaceful means. An unarmed ship was sent into the Bioman sphere but never returned and was apparently callously destroyed. The Dynarx were also contacted but because of their chaotic existence and lack of stable social order very little has so far developed at that front. At the same time, a message was sent to your emperor. Shortly thereafter a reply was received from one Melor Carey, who promised to supply us with all the Dalkanium under his control—"

"Four planets worth!" cried Nolan.

"Well, that is what the message stated. We had no reason—not then—to doubt his sincerity. He asked only that we explain the reasons behind our sudden need. And we did."

"You told him about the clouds?" said Nolan.

"We told him everything I have told you in shared honor this day. He never replied. We sent a second transmission and a third. Still, no reply."

Nolan was nodding. "That's old Carey exactly. Find a weakness and then exploit it. He's a veteran of the art of double-dealing. The population of the Empire is close to one trillion. Of them all, if I were you, the last one I'd ever ask to help is Melor Carey."

"So we learned," Mo-leete said, "much to our sorrow. Further transmissions were also ignored. Then an armed imperial cruiser suddenly appeared within our borders. It conducted a survey of several star systems, all of which lay within the paths of expanding clouds."

"I was aboard that cruiser," Keller said.

"In response," said Mo-leete, "we sent an unarmed ship to speak directly with the Emperor, but the vessel was turned back by one of your patrol ships long before it reached Earth."

Maillard nodded. "Matthew Carey told me something of that, except that, in his version, the ship was armed to the gunnels. I didn't believe him. I knew— or I thought I did, till Tedric and Nolan showed me otherwise—that any Wykzl ship could blast a hole through our entire fleet. I simply believed he was making the whole thing up."

"What about that?" Nolan asked Mo-leete. "Do you think Matthew Carey knows about the clouds, too?"

"I had originally assumed so, yes, but during our meeting on the lifeboat, he indicated that he did not, and I had reason to believe him. His father seems to have confided some of the truth to him, but not all of it."

"Just as well," said Nolan. "But I do wonder why."

So did Tedric, but he sensed that this question would not be answered here. He asked Mo-leete, "But what about Evron Eleven? You still haven't explained what brought you here?"

"Sheer desperation. What else? We desire war no more than you, but we had to increase our supply of Dalkanium and do it soon. We frequently intercept stray communications from your fleet. There are times when our vessels may perhaps intrude somewhat upon your rightful borders. A message came to our attention concerning a rebellion among the Dalkanium miners on Evron Eleven. There was much discussion among us and, I should add, some considerable hesitation. But desperation won out, as it perhaps must. I was sent here in command of our most powerful cruiser to seize the mines of Evron Eleven for the survival of my own species. I have, as you know, failed in my mission. My successors, when they come, most likely will not."

Maillard looked at Mo-leete through narrowed eyes. It was plain to Tedric that the Wykzl had intended his last remark as a threat. "Are you attempting to warn the Empire?" Maillard asked.

"I am. From myself, you have nothing more to fear. Having surrendered according to the proper ritual, I am rendered incapable of further action. But you must understand the solemnity of the situation. We dare not fail to try and try again. The Dalkanium is essential to our existence, like air or blood."

"It could mean a resumption of open warfare between our nations."

"But you could grant our request and thus forestall such an event."

Maillard shook his head. "I'm afraid I have no such power."

"Then who does? Besides Melor Carey?"

"Only Emperor Kane himself. If him."

"Then I must ask you," said Mo-leete. "According to the rituals of our species, you and I are brothers in honor. As such, I beg of you. Act as our intermediary. Go to the Emperor and tell him what I have told you. He is a creature capable of knowing honor. Such we have always believed."

"He is that, true," Maillard said, leaving unspoken the fact that the Emperor's freedom to exercise his capability was severely, if not hopelessly, restricted.

"Then you will grant my plea."

"To prevent a war, I'll try anything. I fought in one war. It was ugly and debasing and I never want it to happen again."

"And you?" said Mo-leete, looking at Nolan.

"I go along with the captain. The Emperor's no confidant of mine, but I'll give it a go."

"Tedric?"

"To the best of my ability, Mo-leete."

"Keller?"

"I'm with the others. Not that anybody like me has ever set eyes on His Highness, but I'm with them."

"You are brothers in honor." From his place on the ground, Mo-leete leaned forward and extended a hand. Again, Nolan, Tedric, Maillard, and Keller linked theirs with his and, again, as a ceremony, it provided a silent, emotional moment for all concerned.

Mo-leete stood up. Bowing, he indicated the others should join him. "Now I will depart and, when my robots complete their task of freeing those imprisoned underground, I will leave."

"That is our wish," said Maillard. Even Carey had dared raise no objection to that. Mo-leete would use the Wykzl battletug to return to his own nation. To have restrained him, held him prisoner, might have constituted an act of war in itself. No one wanted to make the present situation worse than it already was.

"We shall meet again," Mo-leete said. He was facing Tedric as he spoke, and the words were meant as a statement, not a question.

Tedric didn't know why, but he felt as sure as Mo-leete that this was true. "We shall."

Mo-leete turned to go away. He moved with surprising swiftness, mounting the hills of dirt and rock with the grace of a programmed robot. Tedric watched the tip of the alien's head rising and falling up and down the mounds.

When he turned back, he noticed something.

The other Wykzl—the one he thought might be the same one he had captured—had not budged. Silent during the entire discussion, the Wykzl had been forgotten. But now, there he sat—as if he intended to stay.

Nolan had also noticed the same thing. He cupped his hands and cried out, "Hey, what about him! What about this one!"

Mo-leete paused at the top of a hill, a dim shrunken figure already. His voice reached them as no more than a whisper. "He is Ky-shan."

"But what's he doing here?"

Tedric could have sworn he heard a distant, stifled laugh. Mo-leete's voice, when it came, seemed louder, too. "Ask him!"

Nolan looked at Tedric. "Now what's up?"

"I haven't the slightest idea."

Mo-leete had resumed his hasty getaway. He dipped down out of sight and failed to reappear at the crest of the next hill.

Captain Maillard seemed to have some sort of premonition. "I think you ought to do as Mo-leete says. Ask the Wykzl."

Tedric decided there was nothing else to do. He went over to the Wykz and said "Ky-shan. That is your name?"

The Wykzl looked up with wide, blank eyes. The tendrils on his forehead twitched at the ends, as if he were transmitting or perhaps receiving a message. "I am called that, sir." His voice was nearly identical to that of Mo-leete. In the dark, it would have been impossible to tell them apart.

"Are you the same Wykzl we captured and brought to our ship?"

"I am he."

"You are free to go now."

"No."

"No?" Captain Maillard made a sound like a man receiving confirmation of his own worst fears, but

Tedric wanted to hear the truth from the Wykzl himself. "Why is that so?"

"Because I was captured and never surrendered."

"You mean the way Mo-leete did, with the handshakes and everything."

"Yes," said Ky-shan. "It is a tradition among my people. He who is captured without an acceptance of surrender is branded forever as a degenerate and coward. I am that."

"But you can surrender now if you wish."

"It is too late. I was held against my will. It is the same."

"But what will you do now?"

"Stay here. Go with you. The master must command the coward."

"But you're not our prisoner."

"I am your—" he searched for a word to convey his native meaning "—your property."

"But slavery is against all our laws."

Captain Maillard intervened. "I don't think our laws have very much to do with this, Tedric. It was something I should have realized as soon as you appeared on board the *Eagleseye*. We old sailors and soldiers know all about it. If he tried to go home, they would kill him. The circumstances don't matter. It's a law among the Wykzl as firm as any of ours. By leaving Ky-shan here with us, Mo-leete is trying to save his life."

"But we don't need a slave," Nolan said.

"Then leave him here," said Maillard. "That's really the only alternative you have. Bring him up to the *Eagleseye* or let him stay on the surface."

But Tedric was thinking. Having a Wykzl nearby —perhaps, with time, a friendly Wykzl—didn't strike him as necessarily a bad idea. He didn't know for certain what the future held in store for him, but he had had too many hints already that indicated that the Wykzl were involved. Ky-shan might prove to be of great use to him. He wondered if Mo-leete had possibly thought of that, too.

"You won't raise any objection?" Tedric asked Captain Maillard.

"None at all. It wasn't uncommon during the war. The Wykzl wouldn't fight for us, but they never did anything to aid their own cause, either. They can be trusted, which is more than can be said for almost any human being."

"Then he goes with us," Tedric said, making up his mind for the rest of them.

When their shuttle reached the *Eagleseye,* they were immediately confronted by a bristling Matthew Carey, who demanded to know exactly what had been said during every moment of the meeting with Mo-leete. Captain Maillard spoke soothingly, promising a full written report as soon as he had time to collect his thoughts. Carey said he didn't want any written report, he wanted facts, and he wanted them right now. Captain Maillard said he'd see what he could do and

shuffled off toward his stateroom. Carey, barely molli-
fied, rushed away in angry pursuit.

Nolan shook his head. "He didn't even notice our
new guest," he said, pointing at Ky-shan.

"I don't think he really noticed us," Tedric said,
"and, to tell the truth, I don't much mind."

"Oh, give him time. Wait till he gets tired of
trying to drain old Captain Maillard and starts thinking again. Then he'll remember. Suddenly, it'll come
to him. *Hey,* he'll think, *wasn't that a big blue Wykzl I
saw with Phillip Nolan just now?* And then we'll see him.
He'll be down our throats for sure."

"I can wait," Tedric said drily. "And, speaking of
that, why don't you take Ky-shan to our room, find
out what he eats, how he sleeps, make him feel at
home?"

"At home in our room?" said Nolan. "But it's
barely big enough for you and me."

"There's no other place. He can't go with Keller
down to the sailors' deck, and I doubt that we have
enough authority to get him assigned his own room."

"But we won't be able to turn around—or
breathe."

"Oh, I think we'll manage. Maybe the room won't
seem so small now. After being trapped underground, I doubt that anything will."

Nolan nodded solemnly. "I suppose you're right,
Tedric. After that, anything is apt to seem big by
comparison. Ky-shan." Nolan waggled a finger.
"Come on. Let's go. I'll show you home."

Ky-shan, who had resumed his previous silence the moment anyone ceased to address him directly, went obediently off after Nolan. The two of them had gone several meters before Nolan suddenly stopped and turned. "Hey, where are you going to be all this time?"

"Keller and I are going to check something out. We won't be long."

"What? Something important?" From his eagerness, it was plain to see that Nolan had not yet exhausted his taste for adventure.

Tedric said, "No. It's nothing important at all. Just go off to the room and I'll see you."

"It's a secret?"

"It could be."

Nolan grinned. "Okay. Be selfish, if you want. I'll see you shortly."

Once Nolan and Ky-shan had gone away, Tedric took Keller by an arm and steered him off in the opposite direction. They rode a suction tube three decks up, then disembarked and let a winding corridor carry them through a maze of hairpins and cartwheels. Keller, whose curiosity was plain to see, could finally restrain himself no longer. "Can't you give me a hint where we're going, sir?"

"I'd rather not, Keller. It's just an idea I had. Why don't we wait and see if it pans out?"

"You're the boss, sir."

When the corridor passed a sign that said *Medical Emergency Facility,* Tedric beckoned to Keller. Both men stepped off the corridor, ducked through an arch, and let a round door dilate to permit them to pass.

The Medical Emergency Facility was a huge, high-ceilinged room. Dozens of robot technicians darted back and forth between the smaller operational rooms, where the steady hum of machinery could be heard, and the large central bay. There were many patients here, too, easily separated from the technicians by the fact that they were naked and nearly all female.

"These must be the miners," Keller said. "I'd forgotten they were brought up here."

"Only for a time. Eventually, they'll all be sent below with enough supplies to insure their survival. The mines won't be operating again for months at least, but the Carey family still owns legal title to their services."

"Then the rebellion failed."

"Thanks to a combination of the Wykzl and us, yes. But it would never have succeeded in any event."

"Jania said that, too."

"She was right."

"I know, but—" Keller turned his gaze around the wide room. "Is there some reason why you brought me here?"

"I'm not sure." Tedric let his eyes roam slowly through the room.

But it was Keller who saw her first.

"Jania!" he said, standing stock still as if unable to

accept the evidence of his eyes. "Jania—it's me!"

Every eye in the room—technician and human alike—turned toward Keller.

"It's her, all right," Tedric said. "It's Jania."

"It is. It really is." Keller's face was alive with joy. He broke away from Tedric, sprinting across the room. Jania hesitated for only a moment. Then she was running, too. They met at mid-point. Keller threw his arms around his wife. They embraced and kissed.

Tedric left them there. He went back to Nolan and told him what had happened. Later, Jania and Keller joined them. Keller had more than rid himself of the last vestiges of his grief. He seemed like a new man beaming with delight.

"Lieutenant Tedric, how did you know?" he asked. "I thought she was dead. We all thought she was dead. When did you find out she wasn't?"

"Not until you did, Keller. It was just a guess. I thought there was a possibility she might have decided at the last moment to stay behind and help her own people trapped in the mines. If I'd known for certain, I would have told you. As it was, I thought it was best that I say nothing."

"He never said a word to me, either," Nolan put in. "I suppose we should have guessed."

Jania looked almost apologetic. "I thought I was their leader," she explained. "I couldn't just desert them, live while they died."

"But you're alive now," Keller said, squeezing her

shoulders. "You're alive, and we're together."

Tedric knew it wouldn't last. He said nothing—there was no reason to spoil Keller's obvious happiness—but it could last no more than a few hours. Jania would have to return to Evron Eleven. There was no way Tedric could protect her from that. And when it happened, Keller would be hurt again—perhaps more deeply than ever.

Tedric made a private vow: I won't let this rest. Anyway, anytime, he would return here and set these people free.

But could he? Of what use was his vow, vagrant words, without the power to transform the thought into an act?

He did not possess that power.

Would he ever?

10 PRIME!

Tedric lay stiffly in his berth and tried, as he often had the past few days, to gather together the varied experiences he had lately endured and from them devise a reasonable and sensible whole, a complete picture.

It wasn't easy.

The hour, as he lay, stood well past ship's midnight. The artificial air tasted dry and stale against his open lips, and the gentle humming noise that was a constant presence aboard the *Eagleseye* seemed louder and more demanding tonight. Beneath Tedric's berth, Phillip Nolan slept soundly, while in the corner closest to the door Ky-shan stood. Asleep? Tedric wondered. Ky-shan was motionless, and his breath could not be heard.

The problem—what kept Tedric awake—was that he sought a wholeness and so far could find nothing more than the myriad, separate, irreconcilable segments. The Scientists, for example. Hadn't they brought him to this universe to serve some useful purpose? That much seemed obvious. But what? What purpose? Try as he might, Tedric could not decide. It was a mystery—an unformable wholeness. On the course of this voyage, he knew he had expected at minimum to find out that much. He had failed. There were hints—possibilities—but no more. Tedric remained as uncertain of the true reason for his existence as he had back at the Imperial Academy on Nexus.

The *Eagleseye* had departed the Evron system nine common days before. It presently soared through the region of N-space at a velocity (though such a term had no true meaning here) in excess of one light-year per common hour. The ship's destination was the Earth. Emperor Kane himself, it was said, would be there to greet them upon their arrival. Tedric had never visited the Earth. He knew it was the ancient birthplace of all the human races, as well as the present capital of the Empire of Man. Was it possible that he might discover the answers to some of his questions there?

But could he wait?

He decided not and tried, therefore, to reconstruct the crucial elements in his recent life in hopes that, by doing this again, he might discover some clue he had missed before.

He did it without much hope.

He had made friends.

That, as he well knew, was not only a start, it was a dramatic alteration of past patterns. He counted Nolan, Keller, Captain Maillard, Jania, perhaps even Mo-leete and Ky-shan. Something had transformed Tedric in a brief time from the shy, private, deliberately lonely cadet of the Academy into a man upon whom others could rightly depend. It had seemed, while it was happening, like a natural progression, but now he wondered. How could he know that the Scientists had not planned it that way? They seemed to know so much and he so little. He felt like a marionette unable to see the strings that guided him.

If he had made friends, he had also made enemies.

Matthew Carey, for one.

Four days ago, Carey called Tedric to his private stateroom, with none of the politeness and formality that had marked their previous contact. Carey wanted to know exactly what had occurred during the meeting with Mo-leete, and Tedric, of course, refused to tell. He had seen, in Carey's eyes as he spoke, a new awareness that might well have been tinged with fear. Carey knew that something had gone very wrong with his plans for Evron Eleven, and he also knew the people who might have caused that failure: Nolan, Captain Maillard, the rebels themselves. The one person he didn't know and didn't understand was Tedric. And he blamed him. He accused him. He feared him. Tedric could see all of this as the two men spoke, and he knew full well that when and if they again met, Matthew Carey would not make the mistake of underestimating Tedric again.

If he had made friends and formed at least one enemy, he had also learned much and experienced many new things.

He had experienced his first contact with a non-human species. He had visited and seen his first alien star system. He had traveled through N-space. He had commanded obedience. He had saved lives and taken lives. He had seen love.

All of this had indeed occurred—and much more besides—but wasn't that just the same problem again? It was all separate, all disparate—part of the question and not the answer. What did it add up to? What did it prove? Anything? Nothing? What?

Had he learned anything at all about his reason for being there?

He thought not, and that was what worried him.

Then he realized he was no longer part of his own body.

It happened so suddenly and so unexpectedly that he didn't even have time to be surprised. One moment, he lay stiffly on his berth, eyes shut, playing with the same, familiar, disturbing thoughts, and the next, when he opened his eyes, he saw that he was looking down at his own motionless body.

He was floating in the air. He was himself, but he was not blood and bone. He was . . . a spirit.

He felt no surprise. He looked at his body and thought, *I must be dreaming*. That seemed the most likely solution. *I fell asleep in spite of myself and now I'm having a crazy dream.*

Then he floated past the ceiling.

It didn't part. He didn't go around it. The ceiling was as solid as ever. He passed right through it.

But in dreams almost anything could happen, and still he felt no real surprise.

Then he was floating in space.

In the void. In N-space. A vast, thick grayness swirled around him, like a fog. Within it, dimly, he thought he could see the mass of the *Eagleseye*. It was hopelessly distorted, elongated toward infinity. The sight caused his stomach to tremble. He looked away.

Then he realized he wasn't breathing air, because there was no matter in N-space.

Then he realized he was moving through the void at a velocity at least equal to that of the ship itself.

His body—his spirit—was distorted, too. It stretched endlessly away from him front and back. It had no form, no certain corporeal shape.

He shut his eyes (he had no eyes) and tried not to think (did he have a mind?).

He was moving through space at a speed far in excess of that of light.

He was going somewhere.

But where?

Was this still a dream? Was this possible?

For the first time, he wanted to wake up.

He didn't.

Seconds passed. Or minutes. It might have been

days or weeks or centuries. In N-space, time was not only eternal, it was non-existent. There was no ship's calendar to connect him to the normal universe of stars, planets, nebulae, and men. He was a ship himself.

Then the stars were shining.

He couldn't remember opening his eyes (since he had no eyes) but now there was light.

On one side of him (the left?) a billion suns burned. On the other, the lights were fewer and much dimmer. He knew what this must mean. His trip (his dream) had brought him to the edge of the Galaxy.

Only one thing known to man lay in these unexplored regions of space: the planet Prime.

The home of the Scientists.

A bright white sun as big as his fist glowed directly ahead of him. He glanced back and saw that a human shape of sorts had been returned to him. He saw feet, hands, a torso. The white sun grew larger. A small green star shined beside it.

Prime? he thought, and then he knew.

This wasn't a dream. This was real. The Scientists had called him to them.

He floated gingerly down. The atmosphere of the green planet was thick and sweet. He breathed real air again as he glided through white clouds. A bird swept past his head. There was a forest below. An endless, deep, bright forest.

His feet touched the ground.

He felt whole again. He was himself in all respects. The wind touched his face. The smell of wood and dirt teased his nostrils. He was shaking. It wasn't from the cold. The white sun beat down upon his bare head.

A man stepped out from behind a nearby tree and approached with one hand outstretched from his heart.

The man was short, hunched, and dressed in green robes. A crest of white hair topped a round skull. His face was all eyebrows and wrinkes. He said, "Tedric, I welcome you in the name of my brothers."

When he spoke, the man's lips failed to move. He never made a sound.

"Skandos," said Tedric. He clasped the man's hand. It was frail, the grip of a child.

"Then you remember me?" Skandos smiled.

"I . . . I'm not sure," Tedric said. "When I saw you, I knew your name, but . . ."

"But you know where you are?"

"On Prime." He said that much firmly. "And you are a Scientist."

"One of many, yes. Skandos, the histro-physicist. You and I once spent many hours together. You have forgotten, but that is of no matter."

"You were my teacher."

"I assisted you, yes."

"You were the one who brought me here from— from the other place."

Skandos nodded. He pointed to the ground.

"Shall we sit down, Tedric? I am not young and, despite what you may presently feel about my realness, neither am I incapable of growing tired."

"Yes, of course, sir." Tedric sat down. Even though he was quite naked, the bare ground seemed as comfortable as a soft cushion. It adjusted to fit the shape of his rear.

"You have been worried, Tedric, concerned over certain matters."

It wasn't a question, and Tedric responded in kind. "I suppose it's the uncertainty of everything. I feel like a child lost in a dark cave. I recall so little of my life here or before. It comes to me only in snatches. I don't know if I'm doing the right thing, because I don't really know what it is you expect of me."

"What makes you think it's anything at all?" Skandos said sharply.

"Because . . . well, because you did bring me here, didn't you? It wasn't for no reason at all, was it?"

"No, it wasn't for no reason, but I still persist in saying you are mistaken. We want nothing from you. Nothing specific."

It took Tedric a long moment to digest that statement and find that he simply could not accept it. "Then why have you deliberately directed me in every move I've made?"

"Because," Skandos said, and the smile on his thin lips remained, "we have done nothing of the kind."

"But as far back as the fist-boxing tournament, you—"

Skandos held up a hand to interrupt. "Perhaps it will be easier, Tedric, if I simply explain and you listen. We have chosen to bring you here to our world at this time for a number of specific reasons. One such reason is to put your mind at rest concerning what you have just told me. I think, if you listen to what else I have to say, that will occur naturally."

"I don't mean to doubt you, sir. I merely—"

"Then shall we listen?" Skandos arched his huge, thick brows.

"Yes," Tedric said. "Yes, I'm sorry. I'll listen."

A bird sat on the tree branch directly above his head. Its shrill pensive song seemed out-of-place here, an intrusion of ordinary beauty into an extraordinary setting.

"You were brought here," Skandos said, "from another place and time because it was discovered, by us, that your presence in our universe might prove beneficial to those forces which we, the Scientists of Prime, most deeply value. What we did was, I admit, a terrible and pretentious act, a tampering with the actual substance of time and space. I can only defend our deed by saying that it was not undertaken for whimsical purposes. Only the very salvation of this universe would have forced us to act as we did."

Tedric could not keep quiet. "Are you saying that I'm somehow responsible for saving the entire universe?"

Skandos laughed, a gentle sound, bird-like in itself.

"No, nothing quite so dramatic as that."

"Then what?"

Skandos fixed him with a stare. "May I go on at my own pace? I thought we had agreed."

"Yes, of course." Tedric felt flustered. This whole thing seemed so far beyond his own experience or comprehension. "I'm sorry."

"That's quite all right. I understand your concern. Still, I have mentioned our purposes in as much detail as I have only as a prelude to a certain question. One reason why you were brought here now was to learn your feelings regarding your own situation. Tedric, I am authorized by my brother Scientists to ask whether you are now content to stay here or whether you would prefer to return to your original world?"

The question caught Tedric totally by surprise. He had never considered even the remote possibility that there might be a way of returning to his own home. He looked at Skandos to be sure of the sincerity of what he had asked and then, convinced of that, attempted to give an honest reply to the question. "I don't see how I can be expected to tell you that, sir. I remember so little of that other life. It comes to me only occasionally, in dreams. It seems to be a terrible and beautiful world. What can I tell you?"

"I know it is not entirely fair. Your forgetfulness was not deliberate on your part. It seems to be an after-effect of spatial/temporal transference. We never intended that you should not know who you are."

"But it still makes it hard for me to decide."

Skandos nodded solemnly. "Yes, I can well understand. Still, I must ask. Can you answer?"

Tedric thought long and hard but there was never any real doubt as to his reply. "I must choose to stay here. It is my home now. This is real and that other place is a dream. I cannot go back there."

"You can if you wish. If you do, this universe will become the dream."

"No," Tedric said flatly. "I wish to stay."

"Then I will not ask you again. I cannot say your decision displeases us. Nor was it totally unexpected. We feel that you have passed the first phase of your life here. We are glad."

Tedric nodded. He felt glad himself. For the first time, he felt like a true inhabitant of this universe. The burden of his own dim past had gone away. He was a free man at last. "But is that all you can tell me? About your reasons for bringing me here?"

"Now that you have made your decision, no." Skandos wrinkled his brow in an expression of concern. "Still, I am afraid I must be cautious in what I actually reveal. Our enemies are at least as strong as we are. There is an unspoken agreement between us. Pitched war between ourselves and them is too horrible to contemplate. Therefore, we both fight our battles through agents. If I tell you too much, I risk being accused of direct intervention. They, our enemies, might choose to retaliate in kind."

"But who are these enemies? Not the Wykzl?"

Skandos smiled an ironic smile. "No. Not hardly. They are—" His smile faded away. "That is one of the things I'm afraid I cannot reveal."

A sudden flash of inspiration struck Tedric and he spoke before he had a chance to consider the idea. "Do these enemies of yours have any connection with the strange clouds that have recently invaded the Wykzl nation?"

Skandos looked stunned. "You know of the clouds?"

"Mo-leete told me. The Wykzl commander. It was the reason why he attempted to seize the mines on Evron Eleven."

"Yes, I should have known he . . ." Skandos seemed to be murmuring to himself, rather than directing his thoughts toward Tedric. He said, "But Mo-leete surely cannot be aware of the clouds true significance."

"I don't know about that. I was only guessing myself."

"Guessing?"

"Yes, unless it was one of the things you planted in my mind."

Skandos shook his head. "That is another of the reasons why we brought you here. You see, Tedric, we planted nothing in your mind. When you were here on Prime, we taught you only enough to allow you to enter the Academy on Nexus. For us to have done more would again have risked the charge of intervention. We have given you no direct instructions."

"But I—" Tedric could not believe what Skandos said. There were too many moments when he had heard the Scientists speaking as if they stood in the same room with him. "I find that hard to believe. I know it was you."

"No, Tedric, not us, you. Your own keen perceptions led you toward the right paths. There was a reason why you were brought here and not someone else. It was you we wanted—you as a free man. For a puppet, anybody would have served."

"But even at the beginning, even before I went aboard the *Eagleseye,* at the Academy, I remember how I lost that fight to Matthew Carey because you'd told me to."

Skandos shook his head. "That was not us, Tedric. You lost to Carey because you sensed the danger in showing your own ability too soon. You have given us credit for wordless voices that are not our own."

"Are you hinting that I possess some sort of special powers? Am I a telepath? Do I see the future?"

Skandos shook his head very firmly. It was clear he did not feel free to discuss this point. "I will only say that any powers you possess are barely in an embryonic stage at present."

"They will grow stronger?"

"They can grow stronger."

"Then it's up to me?"

"It's up to who you are."

Tedric sat back on his haunches. He knew he had
to accept what Skandos had said as the truth, and yet
this sudden freedom seemed only to make the situation more complex. He felt the overwhelming burden
of great responsibility. "What do I do now?" he heard
himself asking.

"I am not the one to tell you that, Tedric, but this
much I believe I can safely say: do what you can do,
accept your own perceptions. So far, you have done
well. We trust you to continue. Give yourself that
same privilege."

"But I've accomplished so little. I helped destroy
a single Wykzl cruiser, and the Wykzl are not even the
real enemy, according to you. After that, I'm supposed to go out and save an entire universe?"

Skandos saw the humor in what Tedric said and
smiled. Suddenly, tilting awkwardly forward, he
reached out and gripped Tedric's arm. His grasp was
far stronger than it had been before. "I know what
I've told you has only confused and bewildered you.
We expected that would be the case. In time, how-
ever, much that I have said will become clear. Until
then, please do not concern yourself with the fate of
the universe. Worry about yourself, Tedric. Grow.
Expand. Find out who and what you are. Do that, and
you will have done well. I can say no more."

"But—" Tedric began.

It was too late. With no warning, Skandos disappeared. There was no puff of smoke, no rush of air.

One moment he was present and the next he was gone.

Tedric was just controlling his surprise when another startling fact intruded upon his consciousness.

He was no longer sitting on the ground.

He was floating through the air.

The trip back to the *Eagleseye* only repeated in reverse order the sensations Tedric had experienced on his way to Prime. So much had happened to him these past hours (or years) that, dream or not, his ability to express wonder seemed to have been eroded. He swept through N-space like a man asleep. He reached the *Eagleseye* and penetrated its core. He floated in his room above his own body. He dropped down. Body and spirit merged. He was one again.

And awake.

Tedric sat up, blinking. A dream? he asked himself casually. Or had it all been real?

He shook his head.

No, that wasn't the point, he decided in a flash of enlightenment. Something Skandos had said now came back to him and for the first time made real sense.

Tedric now understood that the purpose behind his present existence was nothing more than simple existence. He was here so that he could be here. He must act. That was all.

And this simple fact filled him with such ecstatic joy that he could barely restrain himself from standing, shouting, and cheering.

He dropped quietly down and listened to the

hum of the ship's huge engines. He felt the gentle air against his face. Nolan was snoring, a rhythmic tune.

Things came clear to him.

The Earth was next. The *Eagleseye* was going there now and he would meet Emperor Kane. A victory? A way of saving a universe? He didn't know about that, but he did know it was next.

He faced an unknown enemy, one stronger perhaps than the Scientists of Prime. He knew nothing of that enemy, except that somehow they (or it) had something to do with the Wykzl's clouds.

Should he start there? Fight the clouds first?

But to fight the clouds, he would need the cooperation of the Wykzl and to have that he would have to defeat them in battle and to do that he would have to have a strong and determined Empire behind him.

So perhaps that should be the first step. To bind the Empire together, to recapture the glory of the past. And he knew there could be only one way of achieving that: he must confront the Careys and drive them away from the reins of control.

So perhaps Skandos was right again. Perhaps, on Evron Eleven, he really had begun to save the universe.

It all seemed so simple, so obvious.

It wasn't. He understood that. He faced the work of a lifetime—or more.

He could only begin and hope there would be time. The universe must wait to be saved. Would it?

Tedric slept.

He dreamed.

And, for the first time, he dreamed not of that other place and time but of this place, this time, this world.

He dreamed not of yesterday. He dreamed of today—and tomorrow.

And that, he knew as soon as he awoke, was the real beginning.

END